W9-AWV-248

DR. NO

Also by Percival Everett

DR. NO

A Novel

Percival Everett

Graywolf Press

Copyright © 2022 by Percival Everett

This publication is made possible, in part, by the voters of Minnesota through a Minnesota State Arts Board Operating Support grant, thanks to a legislative appropriation from the arts and cultural heritage fund. Significant support has also been provided by the McKnight Foundation, the Lannan Foundation, the Amazon Literary Partnership, and other generous contributions from foundations, corporations, and individuals. To these organizations and individuals we offer our heartfelt thanks.

Published by Graywolf Press
212 Third Avenue North, Suite 485
Minneapolis, Minnesota 55401

All rights reserved.

www.graywolfpress.org

Published in the United States of America

ISBN 978-1-64445-208-0 (paperback)
ISBN 978-1-64445-191-5 (ebook)

4 6 8 10 11 9 7 5 3

Library of Congress Control Number: 2022930735

Cover design: Kapo Ng

For my editor, accomplice, and dear friend, Fiona.
Thank you for our twenty-seven years together.

Don't go around saying the world owes you a living.
The world owes you nothing. It was here first.

—Mark Twain

DR. NO

Existential quantifier

1

I recall that I am extremely forgetful. I believe I am. I think I know that I am forgetful. Though I remember having forgotten, I cannot recall what it was that I forgot or what forgetting feels like. When I was a kid, my mother tried to convince me that I was forgetful by saying, "Do you remember when you forgot your own birthday?" I think I replied, "How could I?" But it was a trick question. Saying yes would have been an admission of my forgetfulness and saying no would have been an example. "The brain does what it can," I told her. If we remembered everything, we would have no language for remembering and forgetting. As well, nothing would be important. In fact, nothing is important. The importance of nothing is that it is the measure of that which is not nothing. Is nothing the same as nothingness? Students love to imagine such things. There is in fact no nothing; the simplistic argument for this assertion is that the observation of nothing requires an observer, and so the presence of the onlooker negates what might have been pure absence, what might have actually been nothing. If nothing falls in a forest and there is no one around to observe it, does it make a nil? The better argument, one that embodies the simple one and any other, is that one can spell nothing. Parmenides might have been a shabby dresser, but he had a point. The ontological argument might not have worked for the existence of God, but it is indisputable for the existence of nothing. Ei mitään, rien, nada, nicht, nic, dim byd, ikke noget, ingenting, waxba, tidak ada, boten, apa-apa, kitn, nihil, and nenio. Kind of an ontological argument for the existence of nothing.

My name is Wala Kitu. Wala is Tagalog for nothing, though I am not Filipino. Kitu is Swahili for nothing, though my parents are not from Tanzania. My parents, both mathematicians, knew that two negatives yield a positive, therefore am I so named. I am Wala Kitu. That is all bullshit, with a capital bull. My name is Ralph Townsend. My mother was an artist, my father was an English professor who ended up driving a taxi. I am, in fact, a mathematician of a sort. But I use the name Wala Kitu. I study nothing.

I am serious about my study. I am a distinguished professor of mathematics at Brown University, though I have not for decades concerned myself with arithmetic, calculus, matrices, theorems, Hausdorff spaces, finite lattice representations, or anything else that involves values or numbers or representations of values or numbers or any such somethings, whether they have substance or not. I have spent my career in my little office on George Street in Providence contemplating and searching for nothing. I have not found it. It is sad for me that the mere introduction to my subject of interest necessarily ruins my study. I work very hard and wish I could say that I have nothing to show for it.

It was my expertise in nothing, not absolutely nothing, but positively nothing, that led me to work with, rather for, one John Milton Bradley Sill, a self-made billionaire with one goal, a goal that might have been intriguing to some, confounding and weird to most, idiotic to all, but at least easily articulated. John Milton Bradley Sill aspired to be a Bond villain, the fictitious nature of James Bond notwithstanding. He put like this: "I want to be a Bond villain." Simple.

We were sitting in a coffee shop on Thayer Street. It was eight on a Monday morning in November, the semester winding down and so the students who had dragged themselves in there were nearly sleepwalking. I was much like them. I had discovered only recently that I needed a full twelve hours of sleep to function properly but had sat up much of the night thinking about the meeting with Sill. I hardly ever remembered my dreams, which seemed right and fair as I rarely recalled my waking life during sleep.

"What do you mean by Bond villain?"

Sill held a spoon like a cigarette. "You know, the sort of perpetrator of evil deeds that might cause the prime minister to dispatch a double-naught spy to thwart me. You know, evil for evil's sake."

"A sort of modernist villain," I said.

"Precisely."

I stared and stirred my tea. I didn't want to look at him, but I did, realizing, as he came into focus, that he was certifiable. But jolly. He was a pleasant-looking fellow, slightly racially ambiguous, an equine face and tightly curled hair. He was a slight man. "You look too nice to be a villain," I said.

"Thank you," he said. "Appearances are only that."

"Have you ever performed an evil deed?"

"Like what?"

"Have you ever killed anyone?" I asked. "Bond villains kill indiscriminately." I was speaking out of my ass. I didn't know the first thing about Bond villains.

"Some do, some don't." Sill poked the air with his spoon. "Have you ever seen *Goldfinger*?"

"I think so. Let's say no."

"Goldfinger robs Fort Knox."

"Where they keep the gold," I said.

"Where they keep the gold." John Sill looked around, measuring everyone in the room. "Do you know what's actually in the vault of Fort Knox?"

"I don't."

He leaned forward, actually resting his chin on the palm of his hand, like a lover or at least like someone who had known me for more than a quarter hour, and said, "Nothing."

"You mean there is no gold there."

"I mean there is nothing there."

"Nothing," I said.

"Precisely that. I am not telling you that there is no gold there. I'm telling you that there is nothing there. What you have been looking for."

The hair on the back of my neck stood up. Still, I was convinced he meant that the vault was empty.

"I'm telling you that the vault is not empty." As if reading my mind.

"And?"

"You, my friend, are going to help me steal it. I've done my research. You know more about nothing than anyone. How much power must there be for anyone who can possess nothing."

"Listen, I'm flattered," I said, "but—"

He silenced me by lifting his hand from mine and holding it ominously in the air between us. "You won't have to do a damn thing. All I want from you is an ongoing consult. Answers to a few questions. For example, when I open the vault, and I will, how will I know that nothing is there? It's a big vault. If it is full of nothing, then how will I move it? How does one transport such a thing? Does it need to be refrigerated at minus 273 degrees Celsius?"

"You're serious," I said. "Which is not so different from 'you're crazy.'"

"I am that," John Sill said. Another glance around and he pushed a yellow slip of paper toward me.

It was a check. A check with many zeros before the meaningless decimal point. It was a cashier's check issued by the Bank of America.

"This is real," I stated, but it was really a question.

Sill nodded. "All you have to do is advise me, answer my questions about nothing and not with some off-the-cuff shit that you save for graduate students and panels. I can get that shit from anyone. I can get that from any number of books. I want your pure, honest confusion."

"Anything else?"

"Of course, this is to remain confidential. I mean, really confidential, really, really confidential." He caught my eyes with his and for a flashing second he looked like the Bond villain he aspired to be. He scared me for that briefest moment. "Okay? Wink, wink, Bob's your uncle."

"Understood."

"So, you on board?"

"This is for me?" I shook the check as if to see if the writing might fall off.

"That's your name on it."

Indeed it was. Spelled correctly and everything. All in black ink. What else could I say, but "Okay."

I left the coffee shop $3 million heavier and also with the belief that, although crazy, John Sill might have been correct about the military possession of nothing. There was a credible faction of the military complex that believed as I did that nothing was the solution to everything. Where my notion of solution was heuristic, the generals' notion was gladiatorial, bellicose, not nice. None of us knew just what nothing was, but its possibilities were boundless; that much was a logical necessity and therefore true. I recalled being approached some years earlier by two generals from the army whose names I might have heard but certainly didn't remember. I did remember that they looked alarmingly similar, though one was a woman and the other a man. They knocked on my office door, timidly, it seemed, for warmongers.

We discussed nothing in a roundabout, yet truthful way for just more than two hours. They wouldn't tell me what they wanted it for and I couldn't tell them what it was or where to find it.

"What do you think you can do with nothing if you find it?"

"That's why we're talking to you," said General He. "We'd very much like to know, you know?"

"You know nothing," from General She. "That is widely accepted. We want your help. Don't you want to serve our country?"

"I've given this country nothing my entire life. I don't plan to change now."

"What do you mean?" from She.

"I didn't mean anything by that," I said. "Not anything is not equivalent to nothing. You understand that, right?"

"Nothing could make all the difference in the world, we know that much," said General He.

I shook my head. "No one can possess nothing."

The generals shared a look that I didn't understand, in fact their shared look did not even register with me until that day as I walked home from my meeting with John Sill. Perhaps someone could find and harness nothing. I felt a little sick to my stomach, fearful, and somewhat giddy with excitement.

It is postulated that before the so-called Big Bang (like many, I imagine that it was more likely a whimper) the primordial constituent elements were things like helium-4, helium-3, deuterium, and protium. The sophomoric question, but no less vexing for that quality, is where did that stuff come from? And just what is the universe expanding into, through, and/or toward? It is either nothing or a something we call nothing and not that dark-matter bullshit that so many buy into. The theory was not my own, but that of a rather weaselly speculative French physicist named Jean Luc Retàrd, yes, who applied the notion of Riesz spaces and the idea of abstracting the order properties to free continuous functions from the details of any particular space, leading to the thought that if nothing actually comes into contact with something, or non-nothing, then that something will cease to exist. One can see the parabellum implications without much use of an imagination. Most believe, wrongly, that nothing is merely the emptiness between subatomic particles.

Nothingness is not emptiness any more than it is the absence of something, some thing, some things or substance. The actual Big Bang is coming, as what the universe came from is catching up to what it will become. To experience the power of nothing would be to understand everything; to harness the power of nothing would be to negate all that is, and the sad, scary, crucial idea here is that this might well be a distinction without a difference.

My dog met me at the door. He had no choice. That was where I had left him. His name is Trigo and he has but one leg. He is a stout, squat bulldog, even squatter given his missing legs. Trigo refers to his three missing limbs as his nothings. I rescued him, that was the language of the shelter, "rescued," though I prefer "befriended." The workers at the shelter were about to "put him down," their euphemism for murder. I asked if they would kill a person with no legs and they of course said no. I took the dog and his one remaining leg away from that place. Twice a day, when he decides, he does his business and I clean him postwaste. He has a wheelie-cart that he doesn't much like but does pull around for about fifteen minutes in the morning for a bit of exercise. When I take him out for air, he rides on my chest in a baby carrier called a Björn. He is an extremely friendly, if discerning, very jowly, very vocal dog. He speaks to everyone.

Trigo and I walked down the hill to the center of Providence and to the Bank of America, where I stood in line to deposit the check from John Sill.

The stunned teller stared at the face of the check for a full minute. "This looks real," he said.

"I suppose that's because it is," I said.

"Wait here," he said.

"Is there a problem?"

"I have to get this okayed by my supervisor."

"Sounds reasonable," I said.

His name was Theodore, I learned this from his nameplate,

black with brass letters. He stepped away some feet and spoke to a smarter-looking young woman. He showed her the check. She looked past him at me, then again at the paper, held it to the light. They both walked back to me.

"Is there a problem?" I asked.

"I don't know," the woman said.

"What's your name?" I asked.

"Stephanie Mayer," she said.

"My name is Wala Kitu. It's printed right there on the face of the check. It's also printed here on my government-issued passport and again here on my faculty ID and also here above my address on the deposit slip ripped cleanly from my Bank of America checkbook. This is Trigo. He has no ID."

Trigo barked.

People in the adjacent lanes were staring now. The lanky custodian had stopped dusting the floor and looked on as well. Stephanie Mayer initialed the check and gave Theodore the go-ahead. I took my deposit receipt and gave it a close inspection, counting the zeros, and nodded, contemplated seeking out Stephanie Mayer's permission to leave, but didn't.

Outside I stumbled into one of my colleagues, a very young mathematician named Eigen Vector. Her specialty was topology, what else? Like most mathematicians, including me, she fit somewhere on the spectrum and was likely to say nearly anything and so she did.

"My shoes match today," she said as a greeting.

I looked at her Nike sneakers. "Two of them," I said.

"Hello, Trigo," she said.

Trigo spoke.

Eigen attempted a bark herself.

"Beautiful day," I said, noticing as I spoke that the sky was overcast and everything was gray.

"I suppose it is," she said. "Why are you so happy? I ask because you seem happy. I'd like to experience happiness."

"I don't think I'm ever happy, to tell the truth," I said. "Not really sad ever, but not happy."

"Well, you seem happy."

"Who knows, maybe I am," I said. "I wouldn't know what it feels like. Trigo, now he's happy."

Trigo spoke.

Eigen Vector stroked his fat, flat face with the back of her hand. "Soft. So very soft. Fat face."

"He's happy because he still has one leg left."

"I would like my life to be symmetric," Eigen said. "Symmetrical? But I can't seem to make it equal its own transpose."

"Was that an attempt at humor, Professor Vector?"

"What do you think?"

"Nice."

"Kind of you to say so. But you do seem pleased about something."

I nodded. "There is a distinction to be made there, you're right, between being pleased and being happy. One is existential, though I don't know which one." We were silent briefly. "I just received a grant that I hope leads to nothing."

"Grants are good."

I nodded in agreement.

"It's raining, you know," she said.

"Yes, I know."

"Do you ever eat lunch?" she asked.

"Yes, I do," I said.

"Me, too. Almost every day. About the same time every day." Eigen scratched Trigo's face again. "So soft. Fat."

I mentioned earlier, at least I believe I mentioned it, the primordial elements, the seeds of everything; however, this is all, again, question begging. Question begging is a rhetorical concept that has lost purchase in the culture. Poorly educated newscasters, sportscasters, and politicians, pardon my triple redundancy, have come to use the phrase "to beg the question" to mean "to raise a question." To replace the age-old title of the concept with the descriptive "to assume a conclusion" is to at once diminish the value of the rhetorical device and to give in to a general and profound attenuation of cultural intelligence. You will pardon my indulgent aside. It, in fact, comes from nowhere, from nothing. Back to begging the cosmological question. The notion is that the Biggest Bang resulted from quantum fluctuations as the universe came into what we call existence, from a nothing we know nothing about. As beautiful as a mathematical model is, as enchanting as a logical proof might prove to be, these are mere ideas, ether, vapor. My understanding of nothing requires that it first be acknowledged that the acceptance of nothing is more than a philosophical and mathematical adoption of that very useful number zero. The Heisenberg principle is concerned not so much with the location of electrons but with the whereabouts of nothing, those gaps where the electrons are not. And the idea of that empty space as metastable vacuum, Hawking and Kaku always wanted things both ways, which isn't even question begging but a failure of terminal regress. I do not want things both ways; nothing is not something, is not the absence of something, but is nothing. Zero might serve occasionally as a numerical placeholder, but nothing does not. Though nothing might be, tautologically, not anything, it is also not "not anything." It is supposed that nothing comes from nothing, which is to say that nothing yields nothing, which yields nothing, which yields not anything but nothing, blah, blah, yak. Infinity might be boring, but it is profoundly inescapable and, surprisingly, rude. I will spare you and myself any lengthy discussion of zero, as in the face of nothing zero is actually nothing, though neither is it anything to sneeze at.

Who could have known that Euclid would be correct only in space, the fact that earthly application is all Euclidean notwithstanding. The flatness of space makes it a difficult place to hide nothing, especially because space is full to its flat brim of the rest of the universe. Is there other life out there? Don't know. Don't care. Are there other dimensions? No. We seem always to want to imagine dimensions that we assert are impossible for us to perceive, no doubt the same impulse that stuck us with notions of deities, but perhaps in space there are only two dimensions, and let's face it, time is hardly a dimension at all, no more of a dimension than love, dismay, or dizziness. And of our three dimensions, the ones we use for tables, stools, and other people, height, width, and depth are, I imagine, all of equal importance or insignificance and all inadequately named. About time and its lack of dimensional status. Logicians, mathematicians, scientists all worry that their proposed theories will yield a contradiction, the coffin nail of rational thought, but should they be more like theologians and corporate and tax lawyers? That one of your axioms is false is met with "yes, I meant that." It is not enough to show that a statement is false; it must as well be demonstrated that its denial cannot be deduced from the sum of our understanding of the world. Why am I wasting time on this? Time, like nothing, in one way, cannot be seen (being seen is not the same as being observed), and though we have clocks, incredibly precise clocks, time cannot be measured, as one cannot measure any abstraction, convention. Without people there would be no time, just as there was no time before people and will be no time after people. Nothing, on the other hand, is not abstract but the most concrete of the concrete world, and it not only precedes humans and rocks and lava and gases but will continue, if not cause, the collapse of the convention time, the implosion of galaxies, and the evaporation of radio signals projected into deep space by wide-eyed optimists like John Milton Bradley Sill.

Of my understanding and, for lack of a better word, theory of nothing it had been said, as it was said of Hilbert, *Das ist nicht Mathematik, das ist Theologie.* Axioms, postulates, theorems, and proofs bored me into senselessness. My younger, baby self would have quarreled without end with my present stance, but of course I was smarter when young, for what that's worth. Trigo lay sleeping on the table in my lab and I looked at my containers, many shapes, sizes, and materials, full of nothing. I could open none of them, as to open one would have been to empty all. I was asked often to do just that, so as to prove my assertion. Such a demonstrative proof, however, would have at once shown me to be correct and also necessarily wrong. To empty a box of nothing would have been to lose nothing and to have nothing left to show for it. So, nothing doing.

2

Trigo and I walked home. I made us some chow, human and pup, and we sat in the dining room and watched students stroll and pedal by. I told Trigo again about the newfound money. He was not one to be easily impressed, but he admitted that we had come onto a tidy sum and then he suggested that we might need a car. He told me that our new job with Sill would no doubt require some travel and since he refused to fly, a car seemed reasonable. I could not argue with him, he's a dog, so I agreed, pointing out that I had never driven an automobile. How could it be, he barked, then added that I would need a driver's license.

Turns out one needs a car to take the driver's test. Turns out one needs a driver's license to rent a car. So, I decided to buy one. There is no law that states that you must have a license to buy a car, though driving it away from the dealership is met with frowns. I therefore sought out a used car from a private seller. Cars for sale in the newspaper were listed alphabetically by brand and I found myself in a driveway in Cranston looking at a 1970 Alfa Romeo GTV. None of that meant anything to me, but it obviously did to the fifty-year-old golf-shirted WASP who was eager to get, as he put it, a *fair* price, a fair price for a vehicle that he referred to on the phone as his baby.

"I know it's a bright color," the owner said. "It's chartreuse."

"Actually, it's arctic lime, maybe peridot."

"Okay," he said.

His name was Kenneth Peterman and he wore kelly-green trousers and the aforementioned too-tight powder-blue golf shirt with an upturned collar. He smiled easily and constantly. "Here, sit behind the wheel. Feel that leather. Get out for a second and let me start her up for you." He fell in behind the wheel and cranked the engine, letting out a noise himself as the motor turned over. "Listen to that."

"There's some—"

"No, listen to that for a second."

I nodded, listened.

"That's like music."

"How much?" I asked.

Peterman looked at me as if offended.

"Does she have a name?" I asked.

This question relaxed him. "I call her Audrey. My wife hates her." Peterman stared through the windshield. "She hates her, but she wants her. Everyone wants Audrey."

I let my unspoken question hang in the air.

"Divorce," he said. "Avoid it if you can."

"I'm not married."

"A very good first step."

I appreciated his rudimentary logic, but still I wanted to know what he expected for the car.

"Can you believe she would take her just to be spiteful? Shrew."

"No, I can't," I said. "Just how spiteful would that be? I mean, in dollars."

"She won't even drive it. She won't even sell it. She'll give it away as junk, to some lame charity that helps poor children, for a tax deduction. You've heard those damn kids singing on the radio. Annoying as hell."

"The kids?"

"No, my fucking wife, almost ex-wife, she's annoying as hell. Boy, I can't wait to say that, ex-wife."

"How annoying is she?" I asked. "I mean, in dollars."

He paused to regard me as if for the first time. "What do you do for a living?"

"I'm a professor at Brown."

Peterman nodded. "I tried to get in there, but I didn't have the right connections. I'm a URI man."

"Good school."

"Yeah, right. Where did you go?"

"Pasadena Community College," I said.

That made him smile. "I've heard that's a good school, too," he said, almost smirking. "I hear it's got a beautiful campus."

"I don't know. At least I can't remember. I was five when I left there to go to Princeton. How many dollars do you want for Audrey?"

"Thirty thousand."

"Cash okay?"

"What?"

"Will you accept cash?"

"Of course." Peterman beamed. He was no doubt thinking about his wife.

"There's just one thing," I said.

"What's that?" he said, suspiciously.

"I don't know how to drive. I'd like you to teach me."

"Are you kidding me? Did my wife send you here to fuck with me?"

I shook my head no. "I will pay you thirty-five thousand if you also teach me how to use the machine. Do we have a deal?"

"On the level? Machine? Thirty-five thousand dollars. The boys at the club hired you to come over here. Those fuckers."

"No, no, on the level," I said, using his language. "I'll come back tomorrow with the money."

"Right."

He didn't believe me.

"What time would you like me to be here? The bank opens at nine and I can be here at nine thirty. Would you that work for you?"

"Whatever you say," he said. He dropped his head and walked back to his door. "Fuckers."

Peterman didn't come back outside while I stood there looking awhile longer at the lime-green Audrey.

That evening I studied the workings of the internal combustion engine and various transmission designs and read the Rhode Island rules of the roads and highways. It wasn't called that, but that's what it was. The brown, white-lettered Roger Williams Park and Zoo sign stuck in my head and for an hour that was all I could see.

I dreamed of empty sets. I had two null sets in front of me, so to speak. One set contained real apples that were not fruits and the other contained married bachelors. Trigo argued in his usual calm way that the sets were equal, stating the obvious truth that neither had any elements and therefore held the same number of elements. I argued that the sets could not possibly be equal because what one set lacked was not the same as what the other set lacked.

"Are you saying, my dear dog Trigo, that a married bachelor is equivalent to an apple that is not a fruit?"

"Yes, that is exactly what I am saying," said Trigo.

"Let me ask you this, is a bachelor a man or a woman?" I asked.

"A man," he said.

"Okay, is an apple a man?"

"No."

"Then how can the apple be a bachelor?"

"But an unmarried bachelor doesn't exist," Trigo barked.

"So?"

"Neither does your ridiculous nonfruit apple. Nothing is nothing. Nothing equals nothing."

"Hold out your paw," I instructed. I also held out my empty hand. "What is in your paw?"

"Nothing."

"What is in my hand?"

"Nothing."

I nodded. "So, you would say that my hand and your paw are both full of nothing. Would you agree with that?"

Trigo nodded.

"Is my hand bigger than your paw?"

"It is."

"Then my hand holds more nothing than your paw. If my hand holds more, then how can what you hold be equal to what I hold?"

Trigo bit me.

As promised, if not believed, I showed up at Peterman's giant split-level at nine thirty the following morning. He was not waiting in the driveway as he had been previously, so I rang the doorbell. The soon-to-be ex-wife answered.

She looked alarmingly like Peterman himself. She was dressed in tennis whites and her platinum-blond hair was pulled dangerously back, adding further tension to her last, but not final, face-lift. "What do you want?" she asked.

"Is Mr. Peterman here?" I asked.

"Why?"

"I'm here to buy his car."

"You are, are you?"

"Perhaps I should come back later."

She looked furtively back into the house, then back at me, smiling. "No, maybe I can help you."

"I don't think so. Your husband told me that you hate the car and that you're getting divorced and that you're very spiteful."

"He told you that, did he? How did that come up?"

"He thought you sent me to, as he put it, fuck with him about the car, though I'm unsure what that means. Then he said you were spiteful and encouraged me to avoid divorce and marriage. Not necessarily in that order."

"How much is he asking?"

"He called you a shrew. Though I don't see the resemblance. I should come back," I said.

"Don't be silly, Mister—?"

"Kitu."

"Mr. Kitu, that car is half mine. What did he say he wants for it?"

"I have thirty-five thousand with me."

"You have what?"

I said it again and watched her face become even more masculine. For some reason I recalled the joke about the horse walking into the tavern and the bartender asking, *Why the long face?* I laughed.

"What's funny?" she asked.

"He's also supposed to teach me to drive," I said.

"What?"

"I don't know how to drive a car. I offered him an extra five thousand dollars to teach me."

Mrs. Peterman started to laugh, nodding as if understanding something. "Very funny. This is like a double-agent joke, right? That son of a bitch put you up to this."

"Listen, I just need a car. I know how they work, mechanically that is, but I don't know at all how to operate one. Beyond the principles. Your husband didn't put me up to this. I'm going to go now."

"Let me see the money," she said.

I showed her my plastic Star Market grocery sack full of hundred-dollar bills. She appeared to have an orgasm, but I wasn't certain. "I'm serious about buying the car, so if you would ask your husband to call me." I handed her my card.

She looked at it. "Professor Kitu."

"My home number is there. I don't have a mobile phone."

Mrs. Peterman looked at me with a tilted head. "No cell phone?"

"That's right."

"I've never met anyone who didn't have a cell phone." She looked at my card again. "You're a math professor?"

"Sort of. I'm in the math department."

"You must be very smart."

"I don't know how to operate a motor vehicle, so not that smart."

"You want an Alfa Romeo, do you? You fancy classic cars?" she asked, and looked again back into the house.

"Not really," I told her. "It happened to be the first ad I saw in the newspaper. I simply want a functioning automobile. I wouldn't know an Alfa Romeo from a . . . a . . . a . . ." I didn't know another make.

"You know that thing has a manual transmission. And it's real funky shifting from first to second. There's a clunk in the clutch. Did my husband tell you that? I'll bet he didn't. He's a crook."

I shook my head.

"Of course he didn't. He's dishonest. That's why I'm divorcing the son of a bitch. So, you don't care what kind of car it is?"

"I do not."

"That's my BMW right there." She pointed toward a small, dark blue convertible parked beside bright green Audrey. "It's got an automatic transmission. It's much easier to drive and it's only ten years old as opposed to that forty-year-old piece of Italian bullshit. It has low miles. I drive it to my office and back. That's it, to Pawtucket and back. I'm like that little old lady from Pasadena. And like my BIPDIP husband, it's never even been out of the state, not even to Boston."

"BIPDIP?"

"Born in Providence, died in Providence. We actually honeymooned in Newport. I hate him so much." She returned her attention to me. "I'll sell you my car for twenty-five and give you a driving lesson for free."

"Okay. I need a car."

"How did you get here?" she asked, as if suddenly thinking of it. "Bus."

"We have buses?" She tossed another glance back into the house, listened for movement. "You go wait over there by my car. I'll be right out. In fact, sit in it. You'll love the seats."

I did as she instructed. I didn't know what was required for a car seat to be comfortable, but I wasn't uncomfortable. I kept my feet

23

away from the pedals. In very short order Mrs. Peterman was outside with me. She held open the driver's door and stepped away.

"You need to get out and go to the other side," she said. I got out. As I was getting back in on the opposite side, she said, "We can't very well have a lesson here, can we? I know just where to go."

She started the car. The engine was much less loud than Audrey's and I wondered if that was a good thing. She zipped out of the driveway and down the suburban lane faster than I knew the rules of the road suggested or allowed. After a couple of turns and a few miles, she rolled us into the uneven puddle-marked parking lot of a defunct shopping center. One store remained open on the end far from us; three or four cars and a pickup were diagonally parked in front of it.

"Have you ever tried to drive before?" she asked.

"Never."

"How is that possible?"

I shrugged.

"No cell phone. You can't drive. How do you get along?"

"I manage."

She stopped and pushed the gear lever forward. "That's park. Never get out of the car unless you have put it in park."

"Okay."

"Say it."

"Park."

"No, the whole thing," she said. "Never get out of the car until it is in park. *P*."

"Never get out of the car until it is in park. *P*."

She switched off the engine. "All right, let's trade seats."

We did. I put my hands on the wheel and tried to relax.

"Buckle up. Put your right foot on the pedal on the left, that's the brake, and turn the key." The motor started. "So, what did you think of my husband?"

"I don't know," I said.

"Did you hate him?"

"I guess not."

"Too bad. He's a real prick. Keep your foot on that pedal, that's the brake, and move the gear shift"—she touched it—"down to *D* for drive."

"What's the *R* for?" I asked.

"Reverse."

"Can't one drive in reverse?"

"I suppose."

"Then should the *D* actually be an *F* for forward?"

She stared at me. "You might have a point, but put it down to *D*. Now, take your foot off the brake and move it to the pedal on the right."

I did and we took off like a shot. Mrs. Peterman screamed. "Stop!"

"How?"

"Step on the brake!"

She peeled herself off the dash and glared at me. "When you step on the gas, do it gently, softly, slowly. Okay? All right, let's try it again. Gently. Treat it like you would a woman."

"I would never step on a woman."

"That's not what I mean. Touch it like you would touch a woman."

"I've never touched a woman."

Mrs. Peterman laughed. "You're joking."

"Why would I joke about that?"

"How old are you?"

"Thirty-five years, three months, and seventeen days."

"No hours and minutes?"

"Six hours and around twenty minutes."

"Very funny. You're hilarious."

"Thank you."

She looked at me for a few seconds. "Okay, let's try this again. Slowly onto the gas pedal, barely touch it." We moved slowly forward. "Good. Press it a little more. Look at the numbers in the middle. You're going fifteen miles per hour. Turn the wheel to the left to go left, right to go right. Simple, right? Try turning." I turned the car to the right and headed straight toward a light pole. "Watch out for the pole. Watch the pole! The pole! Brake!"

I braked hard but still managed to kiss the pole with the front of the car.

Mrs. Peterman and I got out to look at the damage, a small dent and a long crack. She was irritated. "I suppose you're going to tell me now that you're not buying the car."

"Will that affect the way the car works?" I asked.

"No," she said.

"Then why wouldn't I buy it? Odds are better than good that I'm going to run into any number of things in the near and not so near future and perhaps at a greater velocity. The fact is, I need a car."

"What is your first name, Professor Kitu?"

I was impressed that she had remembered my last name. "Wala."

"Interesting. I like you, Wala. I don't think I've met anyone like you. You're direct and honest, almost pathologically so. I'm Priscilla."

"Priscilla," I repeated her name.

She softened her tone and asked if I wanted to try again. And so we did.

She taught me to turn left and right, to back up, how to park, and, most importantly, how to stop the vehicle without slamming my forehead and hers into the steering wheel and dash. She drove us back to her house where she signed over the title and gave me an unexpected, though easily explained, kiss on the mouth. Mr. Peterman watched us from a bay window, his hands appearing to rip the hair from his temples.

As I drove home, I found myself at a stoplight beside a Providence police car. The two officers in it nodded without smiling and peeled away haughtily when the signal turned green. It was then I realized that I didn't need a driver's license. I was loaded with money because of John Sill and I was certain that any fine I might incur would be far less valuable than the time it would take me to go to the DMV, a place that I had only heard endless complaints about, and where I would certainly pass the written portion of the exam and with equal certainty fail the driving portion. I recalled Mrs. Peterman's kiss. It was not at all I had on those few occasions imagined a woman's kiss to feel. She was rather like kissing a colander, I thought.

3

Infinity means nothing to me. How could it? Nothing is neither finite nor infinite. Nothing is neither a null set nor a member of that set that contains all things that are not something. Things are matter, some things matter, nothing is never matter, nothing matters. Nothing walked into a tavern. What did the barkeep say? Nothing. Why would he? Nothing walked in. Trigo told me that one.

Having parked my new vehicle in the driveway, I went inside and sat in my kitchen, Trigo on the table. "It's almost noon, Trig," I said. "We've nearly run out of morning. A sad thought, morning being my favorite part of the day. My least favorite part of the day is from 2:34 to 4:56 in the afternoon." I drank tea. Trigo chewed on what was called a pig's ear, called that because it was in fact a pig's ear. Pigs are apparently useful. Trigo asked me just who was this John Sill.

Sill was born in Memphis, Tennessee, to a nightclub owner named Loretta Sill. His father died under mysterious circumstances during a sanitation strike when John was negative four months old. Because the garbage was left undisturbed for weeks, the elder Sill went undiscovered for a long time and any evidence that might have been helpful was completely corrupted. That and the fact that Martin Luther King was assassinated the day of his body's discovery meant that no one gave a shit. Loretta Sill, formerly a preschool teacher, bought the Regal Club with the insurance money from her husband's death, the rioting and depression that had followed the civil rights leader's murder having sent downtown real estate prices into a crazy plummet. And though she had little interest in blues music, or music of any kind, or the serving of drinks, alcoholic or not, she turned out to be a talented businessperson. She bought another club, the Flatted Fifth, then three more, the Hot Spot, Tim's Place, and the Mother F. When asked why she kept the name of the last, she would feign ignorance and say sweetly, "My, whatever do you mean?" She owned an entire block of Beale Street. She was called the Widow Sill. The Widow Sill did not hate the fact that women worked as prostitutes on her block, but she did very much dislike the idea that anyone else was making money on her block. In short order the Widow Sill had become the Madam Widow Sill, shortened to Mama Widow. The preschool teacher became a racketeer almost overnight.

In contrast to her business life, Loretta Sill's private life was rather staid, directed, boring. She bought a giant 1900s mansion in Central Gardens, the three-story affair that had been the city retreat of a plantation and slave owner named Rogue LeCou. No one could believe that grand estate was now occupied by the short, slender Black woman who dressed more like Jackie Kennedy than Mahalia Jackson, and her awkward, light-skinned son. This was Memphis.

Young John was sheltered from the dubious action of Beale Street and certainly didn't know that his mother was the biggest pimp along the Mississippi River. All he knew was that he was rich, homeschooled by private tutors, and then sent off to Phillips Exeter Academy in New Hampshire. It was while he was attending boarding school, rooming with a pudgy, cystic-acne-suffering, rich WASP from the Upper East Side of New York, that he received the news that his mother had been shot to death by a man named Sinbad Willis. John had suspicions growing up that his mother was involved in some shady business ventures. One might have conjectured that the name Sinbad Willis belonged to a rival pimp or a slick gangster from Beale Street, but it instead belonged to the Memphis chief of police.

"Sorry, son," the overgrown law officer said to the confused seventeen-year-old John Sill. "I went there to serve your mama a warrant for unpaid parking tickets and she met me at the door with a double-barreled shotgun. I'm afraid I panicked and shot her in self-defense." Twelve times.

Sinbad Willis was not talented in anything but was exceptionally bad at lying and John saw right through him, but of course had no idea why his mother was dead.

At Loretta's funeral, in the Lawrence J. Finley AME Church, a drunken street man talked to John from behind. John could smell the sickly sweet, stale stench of alcohol without even turning around. "Boy, your mama was bound to get it," the man said. "And she got it. Was just a matter of time. Your daddy, he seen too much. She had to know what he seen. So, they had to kill her." When John finally turned around, the man was gone, only his aroma cloud lingered.

Weeks later, John found his mother's diaries. He had never known she kept them. Much of it was details of business, fairly graphic detail that made her business concerns all too clear to John. The prostitutes were all unnamed, called the Samples, referred to by numbers, never by names; however, the clients were all named, often with brief histories or descriptions of their professions, families, idiosyncrasies. It was a particular entry dated April 4 that caught his eye:

This morning Milton came to the school all scared. He said he'd seen a policeman talking to a White man holding a rifle bag across the street from the Lorraine. I asked him why it mattered. Then he didn't come home.

It's about eight o'clock. Neighbor Ginny came by. She was crying. Now I'm crying. She told me that Dr. King was shot, killed right here in Memphis. And I don't know where Milton is. It's not like him to be so late. I'm so upset and scared that I worry I'll lose the baby.

Loretta didn't lose the baby, but Milton never came home. He didn't show up for his job as an elevator maintenance inspector. No one saw him until his empty light-skinned hand was seen reaching from a mound of refuse at the landfill.

Seventeen-year-old John Sill became convinced that Sinbad Willis had murdered his father. And now he had also murdered his mother. He really had no idea what was true, but he was smart, angry, and armed with a book full of prominent names. He also had a fortune, his mother's clubs being successful and her investments proving varied and imaginative. She owned many shares of IBM and many more of a company called Apple, Inc. John Sill studied the assassination of Martin Luther King Jr. He read the accepted story of the movements of James Earl Ray. He studied the rise of Sinbad Willis from beat walker to chief of police. He did all this while learning to run his mother's businesses. He sold the Mother F to B.B. King, who changed the name to B.B.'s, which made a lot of sense. He took the money from the sale and gave it all to the "Samples," hoping they would leave the "life." He did not have much faith in that happening, as they all had names like Cinnamon, Destiny, and Diamond. He held out hope for Ruby. As he became more and more comfortable as a businessman, one with substantial negative information concerning town and state leaders, and more powerful as a public figure in Memphis, he grew more and more bitter about the circumstances surrounding his parents' deaths.

On April 4, 1990, John Sill went to Brushy Mountain State Penitentiary in Petros, Tennessee, to chat with James Earl Ray.

John Sill drove from his hotel in Knoxville the forty miles up Brushy Mountain to the prison. The huge gray notched-roof affair looked more like a prison than any building he had ever seen. The facility had what they called a storied past, but he had no interest in that story at all. He checked in at a desk manned by a chinless, thick-necked guard, having arranged the interview weeks earlier, greasing a number of palms to make it happen. The guard looked at his clipboard, nodded his large head, and spoke into his ancient micro-phone. "Bring up James Earl."

Sill sat at a small table in a room full of small tables. Women sat waiting for prisoners to come occupy the chairs across from them. The men filed in, Black and White, and sat. There was no touching allowed, as the guard in the room announced over and over, "There will be no touching, there will be no contact of skin of one individual with that of another individual, in any manner, there will be no rubbing of feet, unshod or otherwise, under the tables or on top, there will be no accidental knocking of knuckles, nails, or fingers. Any touching in the ways I have de-scribed or any other in some way that I may have failed to indi-cate will result in termination of the visit and a cancellation for one month of any subsequent visits." Deep breath. "There will be no touching . . ."

James Earl Ray was the last prisoner to enter the room. He looked around and his cruel eyes landed heavily on John Sill. He walked over and sat. "They didn't tell me you was a nigger."

"Probably didn't want to scare you."

Ray froze for a moment. "What do you want? You want to know if I was really the one that shot King."

Sill shook his head. "Do you remember a man who saw you talking to a policeman outside the boardinghouse? A Black man."

"Shit, Memphis is full of Black men."

"This Black man saw you with your rifle and you were talking to Sinbad Willis."

"Whatever happened to Willis?" Ray asked.

"He's the chief of police."

"Well, fuck me. He done all right."

Sill watched Ray. He was a small man. In many ways. Before the meeting Sill thought that he would be intimidated in the pres-ence of a murderer, that he would be nervous and afraid of talking to a *hard* man, but he wasn't. He was only twenty-two and he felt no fear. "The man outside the rooming house."

"You know it was Willis who shot that preacher. I bought the gun. But, hell, I ain't a good shot."

"The man," Sill said.

"Yeah, I killed him. He seen us. He had to die. What, was he your daddy or something?" Ray chuckled.

"Yes." Sill looked at the tall, barred window across the way. "Why didn't you tell anyone about Willis and get yourself out of here?"

"Get out of here so they can kill me? I'd rather be alive in here than fucking dead out there."

"Why did you escape, then?"

"I like escaping." He looked around and leaned slightly forward. "I'll let you in on a little something. The fucking FBI planned it all. Hoover was going to kill that uppity nigger someplace, sometime. The government was gonna get him. You can believe that before you believe anything. Am I scaring you?"

Sill stared Ray in the eye and said, "Naw, just directing me. I'll let you in on a little something. You're a speck. You don't scare me, because, as you said, you didn't do anything. Fact is, you're a piece of shit incapable of doing anything in this world. You couldn't scare Martin Luther King. You couldn't scare my father. And you can't scare me. Die in here. Chump."

Ray was red with anger. He lunged at Sill, but Sill didn't move a muscle, didn't flinch, didn't blink. He said, "Thank you for your time. I can tell you this, America will pay. You, I don't care about. It would be like getting mad at a bullet."

"I killed your daddy, boy."

"Yes, I know. I won't take your life. That doesn't have much value. I'm going to take your world."

That was when John Sill resolved to be a villain.

But how to become a villain, a cultural disease, an enemy of the system? For that John Milton Bradley Sill turned to what he knew best: James Bond films.

4

There are some distinctions to draw when considering nothing or at least a sense of nothing, *nihil noema*. I distinguish this sense of nothing from the physical object or embodiment, from the psychological or experienced, from any mental depiction or adumbration and from any logical conception or construction. There is no corresponding idea, form, or picture of whatever it is that I am talking about. Unlike a *real* anvil, the *denotatum* of which will accelerate from a height at 9.8 m/s/s and can break up or break something upon contact, there is not much to say or imagine of *nothing*. In my mind, the imagined flight of the anvil is also true, true perhaps of all the *noema* of anvil. But of *nothing* (why the italics, as I am accentuating nothing or rather there is not a thing that I am accentuating), what can I say? Nothing. Fitting.

As I did every evening, I fed Trigo his second meal of the day one kibble at a time from my fingers. He enjoyed it better that way. In the mornings I let him plow his face into the feedbag I tied around his neck, but we took our time in the evenings. I would afterward read aloud to him until he fell asleep and then on until I, too, was asleep, or so I believed, but as far as I knew I continued reading aloud until waking, having either learned a little or much or, I liked to think, nothing at all.

The phone woke me well after daybreak. It was the department secretary. He and I had an agreement that he would call me every morning I was to teach and I would bring him doughnuts. Much to my dismay I had to go teach my graduate seminar in singularity. There were only three students, but they were eager, enthusiastic, and brilliant, I am sad to say. Give me a stupid student any day. They were the ones who would clumsily stumble into something exciting and, rightly, without any sense of having done so. The smart ones always did the reading.

"Let's return to our discussion of catastrophe theory. Maggie, what do you think might constitute a small change in a nonlinear system? First tell me what a nonlinear system looks like."

Maggie sat up straight. "Any set of equations in which there is one or more variables with an exponent greater than one."

I nodded. "What the hell does that mean?"

Maggie gave me a thousand-yard stare.

"Don't worry, Maggie," I said. "Your response is the correct one. It's nonlinear because it's not linear. I know, that's stupid. Nonlinear is meaningless because everything in the real world is nonlinear. Nothing is linear." I let that sink in.

But it didn't. Maggie smiled, said "I understand," and wrote in her notebook.

Gerald, a nice Sri Lankan boy, said, "And so this is the basis for the so-called butterfly effect."

I feigned vomiting. "Gag me with a backhoe," I said. "Or something equally as large. A skip loader, an excavator."

"A fallen cedar tree." This from student three, an individual who had started off the semester as Vanessa and was now a man named Sam. There was never a change in appearance from Vanessa to Sam, no change in wardrobe, hairstyle, facial hair, or affect, bodily or vocally. Sam just informed us one day that he was now a man named Sam. He said he had no pronoun preference. More than that, and I'm certain it was not merely a veiled attempt to impress me, Sam said, admitting the absence of any discernible alteration,

"There is no difference between the genders. Aside from the fact that I am now Sam, nothing has changed. Nothing stays the same."

"The problem with the notion of small changes in parameters," I said to the class, "is that no change is small, no change is different from any other. Change is change, just as a red speck is no more or less red than a red house."

"What about a change in magnitude?" Maggie asked.

"The change is simply a change. The magnitude, the size, the intensity of a thing might be in many ways different, but the fact that there has been a change at all is what's of interest to us."

"Are you saying that change is a thing?" Sam asked. "Like a brick or a fish? As if there is a Platonic form of change?"

"Yes," I said. "Contrary to popular belief, please accept that Platonic forms actually, not virtually, exist. Change is very much like nothing. But, and this is the good bit, there is nothing like change."

Maggie wrote in her notebook, a tan, extralong spiral notebook. She used an expensive mechanical pencil.

"Stop taking notes," I said. "Don't take notes. That goes for all of you. No notes. Never notes."

"Why not?" Maggie asked.

I smiled at her. "Go ahead, note away. Or not," I said. "I like that you didn't just follow my instruction blindly. *Why not?* is the correct response. Take notes or don't take notes. Believe me or don't believe me. Don't listen to me, for everything I say is either true or false. A kind of liar's paradox, I suppose, but not really. Let me put a more or less philosophical question to you. What is the function of identity?"

"Are you asking if identity is a function?" Maggie asked.

"Sure. Why not? Do you have an answer?"

"No."

"That's a little disappointing. I thought you might. What if I said the function of identity is recurrence in discourse? What we want is to find some kind of sameness of reference," I said.

"I don't get it," Sam said.

"Neither do I," I said. "Let's focus on the fact that identification and identity have nothing to do with each other. The latter is not dependent on the former. You can identify nothing and have no knowledge of nothing."

"You know you sound crazy," Sam said. "It always comes back to nothing with you? Always nothing."

"Yes, I do sound crazy," I said. "Thank you, Sam. You may have identified the problem. My problem. You may have put a concrete finger on a particularly important abstraction and that's not easy to do."

Sam laughed.

"Thank you, Sam," I said.

The lie is the arithmetical axiom that for any x in the world x equals x. It is only faith that allows this as irrefutable truth. Even if I define x as that thing that occupies a particular position in space at a particular position in time. I was fairly certain that man occupying a particular position in space outside my office building was John Sill and so I addressed him that way.

"Hello, Mr. Sill," I said.

"Please, it's John. We're partners, so to speak."

"I thought I was working for you."

"Well, yes, technically."

He was well dressed. In my memory of him in the coffee shop he was not quite disheveled, but he was not a natty dresser. Now here he was, tailored iron-gray suit, thin maroon tie, a maroon handkerchief peeking out from his breast pocket. His oxblood wing tips gleamed. He looked like a supervillain or, worse, an upper-crust English spy, an openly promiscuous and functionally alcoholic heterosexual with an on-and-off-again messiah complex. It was the shoes, the way they were tied.

"Why are you staring at my shoes?" Sill asked.

"Your laces. I am thinking of de Broglie's waves. More specifically, Schrödinger's equation."

"I'm sorry I asked."

"Everything is about motion and momentum."

"Did someone mention momentum?" This from Eigen Vector. She seemed to appear from nowhere. Her shoes did not match.

"Eigen Vector, this is John Sill."

"Enchanté." Sill bowed slightly, but dramatically, and seemed to click his heels without moving his feet.

I was surprised, if not shocked, that Eigen appeared taken with either his appearance or his manner, or both. Not that I was encouraging anything, but I felt compelled to offer some kind of explanation for his presence. "Mr. Sill is funding my research," I said, a strange thing for a mathematician to say, as there is seldom any monetary reward.

"I see," Eigen said.

"Mr. Sill is a billionaire," I said, not impressed with the fact myself, but merely offering what I thought was a useful descriptor.

"It's John," he said. "Are you a mathematician, also?"

"I'm a differential topologist."

"I'm certain I won't understand a single word you'll say to me, but I insist on listening to you speak. Just meeting you, I suspect that you, too, could prove useful to me."

It was clear to me that Eigen was likewise understanding nothing that Sill was saying. It was a conversation that promised to be amusing, but of little or no interest to me. "I have to get home to Trigo," I said.

"Oh, Trigo," Eigen sighed.

"Trigo?" Sill asked.

"My dog. I'll be going now." I stopped. "Wait, John, did you want something?" I asked.

"It can wait." He was paying attention to Eigen.

I wandered back through campus toward home, contemplating very briefly Zorn's lemma, stopping because it was not only boring, depending as it did on the trivial ring having the multiplicative unit one, but also incomprehensible. I didn't understand a word of it, a symbol of it, a function of it, especially a function of it. What was the damn thing for? That thinking sent me spiraling the way I always did, wondering what I was doing with my finite, but unknown, number of days of life, realizing that I was a fraud, that I could talk to my colleagues for hours about things I simply didn't understand, that I could fill a board with a proof that might make them ooh and aah, but had no meaning, no truth, no purpose. And the more wrong the noodling was, the more impressed they were. I was a charlatan. I knew nothing. But given that was my chosen topic, I was a successful fraud, a real, fake expert, an expert fake, a fake with real expertise, an ostensive definition of my subject, an object lesson for myself, a pure construction, and so, because irony is the air I breathe, a real-world example of Zorn's lemma applied.

I was well past the businesses on Hope Street and about to make my turn toward my house on Camp Street when someone called me.

"Professor Kitu!" It was Sam. "May I talk to you?"

"You are," I said.

"Yeah, right. I mean, sit down someplace and talk."

"Okay. I'm just on my way to feed my dog." Sam walked with me. "This is the way to my house."

"I wanted to tell you that this is my favorite class."

"Good Lord, what else are you taking?"

Trigo was just where I'd left him.

"Awwww," Sam said. "He's adorable. What's his name?"

"Trigo."

"Poor thing, only one leg. What happened to him?"

"What do you mean?" I asked. "Here, you can hold him."

"To his other legs. What happened?"

"He has one leg."

"When you got him, didn't they tell you how he lost his legs?"

"I didn't ask. I walked into the shelter, saw his face, and said I'll take him. I have to admit the people at the shelter seemed surprised.

I'm pretty certain they were going to kill him now that I think about it."

Sam covered the dog's ears.

"Don't worry. Trigo and I have talked about this. I'm glad they didn't kill him. I think he's happy about it, too."

"I'm sure."

"Tea?"

"Okay."

Sam stepped to the doorway and looked into the living room.

"What you expected?"

"I thought there would be more books."

"Books are heavy."

"Do you move a lot?"

"No."

Sam came back and sat at the table. Trigo licked Sam's face.

"What do you want to talk about?" I put on the water and took Trigo's food from the cabinet. "You can just put Trigo on the table."

"My parents," Sam said. "They think I'm wasting my time studying math. My father's a chemical engineer and my mother is a surgeon and they think I can't do anything with a math degree."

"Well, they're right." Sam looked surprised. I sat and fed Trigo his first bite. "Some people want to do big things in the world. Build bridges, save lives, that sort of thing. Your parents. Some people want to understand big ideas. Will it matter to anyone anywhere that you know the difference between the Knaster-Tarski fixed point theorem and the Tarski fixed point theorem? No, it won't. But it will matter to you."

"Are you happy doing what you do?"

"What is it you think I do?"

Sam was caught off guard by the question.

"I'll tell you what I do, Sam. I do nothing. I try to do nothing. Turns out it's harder than it looks. Not that I know what it looks like. You like puzzles, I know that. This is a great place for your brain to be. You can figure out some of this stuff and explain it to me. I always appreciate all the help I can get."

The kettle called. "Can you pour the water? I'm feeding Trig."

Sam stood and walked to the stove. "I don't know what you're saying."

"If it weren't for Gödel, where would we be?"

"I don't know, where would we be?"

"I don't know, either. Perhaps in service to a bald present king of France."

"What?"

"You probably shouldn't seek life advice from someone like me."

"Are you happy?"

"What is happy? Define your terms. This happy you speak of, is it a state or a condition, if there is a distinction to be made there? Is it something I can take on, something that I can occupy, or is it something that occupies me? Is it something I find or something that I passively catch?"

"Are you satisfied?"

"Are you begging the question?"

"Are you making fun of me?"

"No, I'm not. Do I seem happy to you?"

"As a matter of fact."

"Then I suppose I am. What about me looks happy to you?"

"You're, like, in your own world all the time. No one seems to bother you. Nothing seems to bother you."

"Actually, nothing bothers me all the time. Some things we have to keep straight. But I know what you mean. You're not seeing happiness. You're seeing social awkwardness, a mild blindness to the normal range of social cues. You like me because I'm weird and you like that because you think you're weird. And you are, in a good way. You know what a homotopy equivalence is and you don't need to know that. No one needs to know that. Face it, that's weird." I drank my tea.

"I don't know what a homotopy equivalence is," Sam said.

"Neither do I, but you know what I mean."

"So, should I switch to applied math or physics the way my parents want?"

"Ouch. If you want to. If you don't want to, don't. Life is finite, often more finite than anticipated. If you like to be in your head, be there."

"Thanks."

"Feed Trigo a bite. It will make you happy."

A canister came in through the open kitchen window. Sam and I looked at it. It was silver in color with blue lettering. *Riot Control*, it read. We looked at each other and then the thing began to hiss and emit white fog.

"What do you think that is?" I asked.

"Tear gas?"

The kitchen door flew off its hinges. Trigo barked. I scooped him from the table into my arms. "Professor Kitu?" Sam's voice was scared, high. Men in black body armor stomped into the house. It was hard to see because of the smoke and the burning of my eyes. "Get down on the floor," Sam said. I did and I could see a little better. Big black boots came together in front of me. I looked up into the fog. I felt a sharp and sudden pain on top of my head. I felt Trigo fall from my grasp.

5

I awoke to a bright light in my face. Quickly, I was aware of two bright lights and then three. I tried to raise my hands to shield my eyes but could not. While my eyes adjusted to the brightness, I could see that my wrists were shackled to a metal table. My ankles were as well shackled to the metal legs of the chair. My throat was scratchy, dry, tight. I was thirsty. I was hot and sweaty. I couldn't see past the lights so I closed my eyes and tried to listen. I could hear only the buzz of the fixtures.

"Where's my dog?" I asked.

Two of the florescent bulbs went black with loud clunks that seemed somehow old fashioned to me.

"Don't you want to know where you are?" a man asked.

I looked up and was surprised to be able to see the man and his face. If he had looked more ordinary, he would have been invisible. If it was at all possible for a suit, ill-fitting or otherwise, to be colorless, this was it. "I know where I am," I said.

"Do you?"

"As a matter of fact. I'm here with you. I do want to know what's been done with my dog."

"Do you, now?"

"And my student. My student was with me. Where is Sam?"

"Don't you want to know why you're here?" the man asked.

"What exactly do you want me to want to know? Again, my student?"

"We'll get to that," the man said. "My name is Bill Clinton."

I looked at him, head tilted.

"Not that Bill Clinton." He had seen my questioning expression before. "I work for a government agency, but I can't tell you which one."

"It's top secret," I guessed.

"Yessireebob."

"FBI?"

"Nope. That's not secret."

"CIA?"

"Nope."

"NSA?"

"Nope."

"DOD?"

"Nope."

"DEA?"

"Nope."

"EPA, PTA, NRA, CNN?"

"You'll never get it," Clinton said.

"I've only started. Given there are twenty-six letters in the alphabet and that there is no reason for me to assume that your agency has three initials, but could have one, two, three of twenty-six, then I have thirty-seven million more guesses coming to me. So, let's start again. A?"

"Shut up!" he barked. "You're a wisenheimer."

"Where is my dog?"

"In due time." Clinton tossed a four-by-six-inch black-and-white photograph onto the table in front of me. "Do you know this man?"

"I have seen this man."

"I asked you if you know him."

"I know his name," I said.

"Who is he?"

"You might call him my patron, my benefactor, perhaps even my employer. My sugar daddy. I heard that used in a movie once. Though I don't know what sugar has to do with anything."

"I'll tell you what sugar has to do with anything. He gave you a check for two and a half million smackers. That's a lot of cabbage."

I was taken with his language. "More like Boston lettuce, in that it was three million, but go on," I said. "Bok choy? Romaine."

"A funny guy. What was that money for?"

"Nothing, if you must know." I told the truth.

"Listen, you're dealing with the federal government here. I want to know what that money is payment for."

"I told you. Nothing."

"What's his name? The man in the photograph."

"You apparently know his name," I said. "Where's my dog?"

"Do you know where John Sill is now?"

"Who?"

"John Milton Bradley Sill. The man who gave you the moolah, the do-re-mi. The gent in the pic."

I couldn't keep from smiling.

"You find this amusing." It was a statement and I agreed with it, and as this was an assertion I felt no need to respond.

"Well, do you?"

"Where is my dog?"

"Hot in here, isn't it. You must be feeling pretty thirsty right about now. I bet you could go for a little something to wet your whistle. Ice water, a nice icy soda pop, a nice tall glass of frigid sweet tea?"

"Is it wet one's whistle or whet one's whistle?" I asked.

"What?"

"Wet is the one that makes sense."

"Shut up."

"You know, when we handle propositional attitudes with intensional abstraction, as we are sort of doing here, their opacity becomes, shall we say, localized in that of intensional abstraction."

"What are you talking about?"

"I told you, nothing. Now where is my dog? His name is Trigo. He's remarkably resilient and if you just bring him to me we can be done with this little episode in a, as you might say, jiffy."

"Mitchell." Clinton stepped away and spoke to a man who stepped forward. "He's crazy," he said. "I can't get anywhere with him. You try."

Into my view stepped Mitchell, who, except for the fact that he was Black like me, looked alarmingly, terrifyingly, like Clinton.

"How're you doing?"

"Well, and you? Where's my dog?"

"You see we have a bit of a problem with such large deposits from individuals that our government considers possible terrorists. That always sends up a red flag. Now if you could only tell us what that payment was for?"

"I can tell you, nothing. Why a red flag?"

"Is my partner right? Are you crazy?"

"Once more propositional abstraction proves opaque."

"What?"

"If you won't tell me where my dog is, his name is Trigo, then tell me where you've taken my student."

"She's fine."

"He."

"He?"

"Or she. They."

"We let your student go. We scared the hell out of her, him, them, and then he, her, them was sent home."

"My dog? Did you scare the hell out of him?"

"What is Sill up to?"

"You realize I'm just a math professor. I don't even use a computer."

"Yeah, and Lee Harvey Oswald was just a, just a . . . Clinton, what was Lee Harvey Oswald?"

"An assassin."

"Before that?"

"A pinko."

Mitchell's mobile phone rang and he answered it, listened intently, nodded, then put it away. "Professor Kitu, you can go."

Clinton stepped forward.

"Director said to let him go," Mitchell said.

"Just cut him loose?"

"Unhook him."

Clinton talked while he unlocked my cuffs and ankle shackles. He smelled like hairdressing cream. "Just know that we'll be watching you. We're going to be on you like a cheap suit."

"My dog?"

"Give him his damn dog!"

6

Someone who might have been standing behind me the entire time put a scratchy cloth sack over my head. I was roughly walked out of that room into a corridor. I could tell by the hollow sound of our footsteps. It became clear to me in short order that they were walking me in a circle through the same hallways. Even a mathematics professor knows that four equidistant right turns land you where you began. I felt the cool outside air on my hands and neck and the cover was snatched from my head. It was dark out, but I could see that I was in Fox Point, the Seekonk River in front me. My favorite Portuguese bakery was just a block away and I would have stepped inside had it been open. It took me only thirty-seven minutes to walk home and there I found a confused, perhaps angry, certainly terrified, Sam sitting on my stoop with Trigo aboard lap.

"Are you okay?" I asked.

"What was that all about?" Sam asked.

"Did they hurt you?"

"No."

"Have you been sitting here all this time?"

"I couldn't leave your dog."

"Thank you."

Sam asked me his initial question again.

"Top-secret government agents having a casual chat with me."

"Why?"

"That is a very good question for which I do not have a very good answer, either for you or for myself. Trigo is comfortable with you."

"He's great. He took a shit in my lap."

"Well, he can't walk."

Sam nodded.

"It's late," I said.

"That's it? Tear gas, men with guns, kidnapping and you tell me it's late? Should I keep this to myself? I'm scared. I thought they were going to kill you. Is this what a degree in math gets you?"

"I don't know. It's never happened before. I'm sorry they scared you."

"Should I continue to be scared?" Sam asked.

"I don't know, Sam. I am pleased to report that apparently they're not interested in you."

"Yet."

I nodded. "Yes, that's a reasonable point." I took Trigo into my arms. "But it is late and you should go home."

"Can you drive me?"

"I don't think you'd like that. Can you drive?"

"Yes."

"Take my car and bring it back tomorrow."

I watched Sam drive away, rather expertly by my standards, and then went into my house to send an email to John Sill. That was my only way of reaching him. I assumed my email was being monitored and so I was decidedly cryptic:

Dear John,
Would like to suggest that Frege was puzzled. A large bird resembling an eagle has landed on my roof. I recommend that you read Bayes' rule. The weather in Monaco is fabulous this time of year.
Unsigned

In a matter of seconds Sill responded:

Dear Unsigned,
Understood. Go about your day. Put on a good face.
Yadda, yadda, yadda.
John

A second email followed.

Isn't this fun?

There was a song attached (a woman singing a cappella):

They said he wanted money
But this was hardly true.
They saw him in a kayak,
But he escaped in a canoe.

Round, round he goes
The sun, the moon, the park, and back
To where he started, to what he knows
To what he has, to what he lacks.

Down to the river, he said he courted power
The kind reserved for God.
Not enough to be impressed,
He wanted them all awed.

Round, round he goes
The sun, the moon, the park, and back
To where he started, to all he knows
To what he has, to what he lacks.

They said he was a danger
A villain and a foe
But all the plans they feared
Were the ones they'd never know.

Round, round he goes
The sun, the moon, the park, and back
To where he started, to all he knows
To what he has, to what he lacks.

I wrote back.

Dear John,
That was a terrible song that I didn't understand.
Wala

I looked out the window of my bedroom and saw the cliché black sedan parked across the street. I imagined the face behind the wheel to be that of Clinton, but in truth I could not see any part of him. I also imagined them eating burgers and fries, perhaps enjoying pizza and milkshakes and I found myself hungry. I put Trigo in the Björn and walked out of the house. My plan was to walk past the university and down the hill to the all-night diner called Allnight Diner, where I might enjoy a burger and fries, but not likely as the food there was barely edible. It was, however, open all night. I wondered how the feds might follow me, out of the car or in it, driving a few meters at a time perhaps. I didn't help them, as I used my usual route, cutting through the playground, walking against traffic on a one-way street and finally through the front door and out the back of a long-defunct doughnut shop, once called Doug's Doughy Doughnut Dungeon.

In the Allnight Diner I sat by the window and searched the street for my followers or their sedan, but they didn't show. John Sill, however, did appear. More surprisingly Eigen Vector was still with him, but she was dressed in a strange way, not at all like herself, not at all like a topologist or even one who does applied math. She was wearing a skin-tight black jumpsuit and black leather high-top sneakers that matched.

"Eigen?"

"What do you think?" she asked. "The new me. The old me unveiled. That's how I like to think of it."

"What have you done to her?" I asked Sill.

"Nothing. This was all her idea. We're partners now, she tells me. It all happened so fast. She's very smart, as you know, and, I might add, pretty damn persuasive. Don't argue with a topologist. That's what I always say. Well, not really. Never said it before in my life, but I will from now on."

"Partners? What does that mean, partners?" I looked to Eigen's eye shadow for an answer.

"I want adventure," she said. "Wala, do you remember the excitement you felt when you were a kid and you finally understood Gödel's proof?"

"Yes."

"Well, I want something far better than that. I want my heart to race. I want to sweat, not just perspire, but sweat."

"Run around the block," I said.

"You know what I mean."

"So, what is it you're telling me? What do you plan to do?"

"I plan to be bad."

To Sill, I said, "I take it you know all about my interrogation."

"I know they came for you. Did you tell them anything?"

"What is there for me to tell? They already know you gave me money, though they had the amount wrong. They wanted to know why you paid me and, frankly, I wouldn't mind knowing myself. I told them you were interested in nothing, but that merely confused them. Much like I'm confused right now." I turned my attention back to Eigen. "What do you mean by *be bad*?"

"You know, bang, bang, stabby, stabby, spy stuff."

I looked at Sill. He smiled and shrugged. "That was Eigen singing by the way. The email."

"Yes, that was my *terrible* song," Eigen said.

"Well, it was kinda bad. I didn't understand it."

"What's to understand? It's a song."

"It's got words, right? Well, those words didn't make sense." Trigo barked. "See, Trigo agrees. Who's the *he* in the song? Him?" I nodded to Sill. "*Round the moon?* The moon moves around Earth and it doesn't rotate."

"It's a song."

"Please, please," Sill said. "We can argue about this later. Or not. Right now you need to finish your burger and then we need to get to the airport. My jet is fueled up and ready to go."

"Where are we going?" I asked.

"Miami."

"Why?" I asked.

"To do some bad stuff," Eigen said.

"Why am I going?" I asked.

"For company," Sill said. "By the way, I put another million or so in your bank account. I think that will stir up a bit more interest in you. Also, I might have hidden a couple of cell phones in your house, with calls in the history to known international terrorists and the dons of a couple of drug cartels."

"This is blackmail," I said. Trigo barked.

"More like persuasion." Sill ripped a paper napkin, but not all the way through, and set it on the table. "Shall we?"

I pointed at the napkin. "Is that supposed to mean something? Why didn't you tear it all the way in half?"

"I got tired."

"Why are you doing this to me?"

"Because he's bad," Eigen said. "He's real bad. It turns out I like *bad*. Who would have thought that? I mean, this morning I was concerned with norms and pointwise convergence and tonight, who knows, I might kill someone."

"Well, keep a good thought."

I went with them. I had nothing to lose.

Miami

1

John Sill's Bombardier Challenger 350 was obviously a source of pride. I let my body weight and the weight of the day sink into the white leather seat. Trigo was next to me in his own chair. He was unfazed by the situation, as was his wont.

"I hope you'll be comfortable," Sill said. "It's not the biggest jet. I didn't get the 650 because, well, it's a bit ostentatious."

"I'm very comfortable, thank you," I said.

The flight was very smooth. I slept. I slept a lot in those days, though not always at night. I was a big dreamer, though I was not certain they were always mine. During this flight, however, I don't think I dreamed. I awoke to find my hand on Trigo's snoring belly and my eyes on Eigen sleeping across from me. Sill was seated beside her and his eyes were wide open and focused on me.

"How does one become a billionaire?" I asked.

"Greed." He smiled. "It helps if your mother leaves you twenty-five million in stocks and who knows how much in real estate. She bought apartment buildings and strip malls and parking structures in every city along the Mississippi and beyond, some three hundred properties in total. Then there were the books. My mother collected first editions of everything."

"Books could amount to that much?"

"No, but they set my table. She taught me to learn. Sounds like a load of crap, I know."

I shrugged.

"She was a pimp, you know. Her prostitution business quickly grew from the low-rent variety of Beale Street to expensive call girls in Saint Louis, Los Angeles, Chicago, New York, and especially Washington."

"I didn't know there could be that much money in sex."

"Not the sex per se," he said. "The clientele. The call girls found out from their johns about public projects and programs and my dear mother would then buy the properties and sell them to the cities. Information, Wala, information is everything. And then there was the extortion."

"Your mother sounds like quite a gal."

"She had that American spirit. And she hated America. America killed her one true love. My father. I don't know squat about him, but I know, she knew, everybody knew that America killed him." Sill beamed with an incongruous smile.

"You're a terrorist."

"Of a sort."

"You also hate America?"

"Killed my father. I'm a dismantler. America killed my father and my mother. And nothing is going to change that."

"You mean *nothing*."

"Precisely."

We set down with remarkably little bounce at just about sunup at the Miami-Opa Locka Executive Airport. I knew this because of the sign. I never saw the pilot. We disembarked and were spirited, a word I employ with some irony, away in a nondescript car that might have been a rental, a midsized Japanese sedan. I sat in the back seat with Trigo. Sill drove while Eigen sat beside him, her window open, the wind filling her hair. She looked so, so well defined, if a little trashy. The well-dressed pair were so different from me.

I realized that my belt was a striped necktie that I had fed through the loops of my trousers and that I was not wearing socks. I imagined the color of my missing socks to be black, a primitive notion in the technical sense, but like all foundational, unprovable assumptions it must have meant something about me, but I didn't know what. I was left in the back seat, stroking the fur of my only friend. I admitted to myself, once again, that I was, if not stupid, at least profoundly astray, adrift.

The freeway was packed, barely moving, but moving. Finally there was water. We crossed Biscayne Bay and drove down the middle of Miami Beach, then from MacArthur Causeway turned onto a small road.

"This is Star Island," Sill said. "One way on by car, but there are ways on and off by other means." He drove us onto a property that featured a prominent helipad on the expanse of a meadow. A shiny red-and-white helicopter sat on the pad.

Sill looked at me in the center mirror. "Over there is my Airbus H155. But I'm sure that means nothing to you. Fastest civilian helicopter in the world. You can see I'm fond of things that fly."

I nodded.

"Why didn't we take that from the airport?"

"I find the freeway inspiring," Sill said. "It keeps me angry."

Eigen looked at him adoringly. Trigo rolled his eyes, then produced a bowel movement. "Do you have anything else that flies?" I asked.

Sill stopped the car and set the brake. "That's it. I'm impressed that you're not impressed."

I sensed that I was supposed to be impressed by his appreciation of my lack of regard for his expensive toys. Weirdly, I was. I felt somehow manipulated.

Eigen slipped out of the car as if she and Sill had a long history. I followed them into the modern glass-and-stone mansion, into a massive, nearly unfurnished, mostly marble foyer. There was one large throne-like chair against a far wall.

We were met by a tall, broad-shouldered White servant. "Welcome home, sir," the man said to Sill, taking his attaché case.

"Thank you, my dear DeMarcus," Sill said. "Eigen, Wala, this is DeMarcus. He will take care of whatever you need or whatever you want, for that matter. DeMarcus, show Professor Kitu to his room."

"Of course, sir." DeMarcus nodded to me. "Professor."

I followed DeMarcus through the halls to a bedroom with a veranda that looked out across the water to Miami Beach and a smaller island in the middle of the bay. I stood outside and let Trigo enjoy the sun. There was a monument of some kind on it. "What is that?" I asked.

"Flagler Memorial Island," DeMarcus said. He had a silky-smooth English accent. "No one lives there. No one."

"And over there?"

"That would be the Mondrian Hotel. Very posh. Many people live there. See them having fun along the beach."

If there was resentment or even irony in his voice, I could not detect it. It was as if he were merely, dispassionately giving me information, stating empty facts.

"I assume they are all quite wealthy," I said.

"No doubt. Will there be anything else?"

"Is there a library?"

"A rather extensive library. Would you like me to show it to you?"

"I'll find it."

"Very good, sir. If you need me, just call out my name. I will come."

"Just like that?" I asked.

"Precisely like that."

"DeMarcus."

"Sir?"

"Your name?"

"Yes, sir?"

"Were you born with it?" I asked.

"Professor, no one is born with a name."

"True. Did your mother give you that name?"

"Mr. Sill gave me this name."

"I see. And this is Trigo."

DeMarcus nodded to Trigo. "Anything else, Professor?"

"Yes. Call me Wala."

"As you wish." He paused. "Wala. Mr. Trigo."

When DeMarcus was gone and my door was closed and I was seated on the plush veranda with Trigo in the morning sun, I contemplated the rather fantastic revelation that no one is born with a name. And no proper name was a rigid designator, as it seemed all too clear that there were no other possible worlds, though I might have capitulated to the notion of possible futures, allowing that no future actually existed.

2

I found my way to the library by myself, wandering first through a noisy video game room, several living rooms, two remarkably well-equipped kitchens, an indoor basketball court, and a theater with rows of red velvet chairs, each room gaudier than the last. The library, however, was beautiful, incongruous with the rest of the mansion. It had three twelve-foot-tall walls of books and the fourth wall was all glass and looked out onto an infinity pool and the bay beyond.

The collection was nothing less than magnificent. The first book I saw, placed safely in a Lucite case set a meter off the floor on a pedestal, was the *Codex Leicester*. The yellowed paper was like gold, the script of da Vinci barely readable, but as clear as the boldest type. Across the room was a 1440 Gutenberg Bible. On the shelves I found one treasure after another. A first edition of Newton's *Principia*, a nice start, followed by *Über eine Eigenschaft des Ibengriffes aller reellen algebraischen Zahlen* and *L'anneau d'homologie d'une représentation*, crazy enough, but then works like Euler's *Recherches sur la courbure des surfaces* and Riemann's *Über die Hypothesen, welche der Geometrie zu Grunde liegen*. I was sitting in a very comfortable leather chair with Gauss's *Disquisitiones generales circa superficies curvas* in my lap when Eigen Vector walked in. She was dressed in red this time, another bodysuit. No shoes and so they therefore matched.

"I've never seen anything like this," I said. I was referring to the books, but I could just as well have been talking about Eigen.

"He's amazing."

"I agree."

Eigen paused, having a thought. "Our poor students," she said.

"My seminar is next week. I have no plans to miss it."

She stared at me briefly, perhaps with contempt, certainly judgmentally.

"What?" I asked.

"I teach three times a week. You teach once. Why is that, Wala? I know my math inside and out, backward and forward, derivatively and integrally, and I teach all the time. You understand no math and work on nothing."

"True."

"I don't get it."

"You're right, Eigen. I know nothing and for that I am well compensated. You know a lot and receive less. I'm a terrible mathematician. You know, it could be sexism."

"What's that?"

I looked at her disbelievingly for a few seconds. "Prejudice and discrimination against someone because of his or her gender, usually hers."

"That's a thing?"

"Pretty big thing. It's been going on for quite a while now, as in forever. It's been in the newspaper from time to time and on occasion made clear." I didn't mean to sound sarcastic, not very sarcastic.

"That doesn't seem fair."

"No, Eigen, it's not. That's sort of the point. Neither is racism."

"Don't tell me."

I nodded.

"The world is just a horrible place," she said. "I've been locked up with equations, theorems, and proofs my entire life. What a terrible place we live in. Well, anyway, John is going to take care of all that."

"What do you mean?"

"Nothing," she said.

I closed the Gauss. "I can't believe the books in here. Do you know there's a Shakespeare and Company edition of *Ulysses* over there? Number one."

"I don't even know what that is. I've been sheltered, Wala, walled off, closeted, imprisoned. Good God. How is it you know this stuff?"

"I know nothing," I said.

"What is it with you and nothing?"

"Every child does that experiment with gas and heat and charts that line down to zero Kelvin, minus 273.15 degrees Celsius. Well, when I was five and performed the simple experiment and drew my graph, I realized that only the line itself would ever actually get down to that physically unattainable temperature. It was a magic trick of sorts. But simple reason led to me understand that, theoretically, not only should matter disappear at that point, but that there should be no bringing that matter back. Nothing yields nothing."

"So?"

"Where does it go? How can something disappear without a trace? The universe is supposedly a closed system. No release of energy or anything, just gone. Nothing. I realize that some people say there is simply a lack of particle movement at that temperature, a temperature you can't get to, and there are probably small fluctuations, but that's just trying to avoid where reason leads."

"You sound like a physicist," she said.

"There's no reason to be insulting."

"I don't understand any of what you're saying. I don't care. I don't find any of that at all interesting. Plus, I think you're just making it up. I think there is nothing there."

"That's what I've been telling you."

"Phooey. I'm still thinking about this sexism thing." With that, she stomped out of the room, her matching naked feet slapping the marble floor.

3

I was napping. I sat in a chair on the lawn, the bay at my feet and, in my lap, *Historiae Aethiopicae libri decem, nunquam antea in lucem editi* by Heliodorus. I didn't have the energy to read the Greek, but I let the Latin dedicatory put me to sleep. The age and weight of the slim volume caused my muscles to relax.

"What have you there?" Sill asked, waking me.

"A very old novel," I said. "I hope you don't mind. DeMarcus said I could bring out any book I liked."

"Of course."

"Where is your dog?" Sill asked.

"Fat face," Eigen said.

"He's lying in the sun on the veranda. He looked so comfortable that I couldn't bring myself to move him."

"Are you ready for some lunch?"

Eigen was dressed in tennis whites now, with white sneakers that again matched.

"You look sporty," I said.

"I am," she said. "I have a lesson after lunch."

I turned around in my chair to see that DeMarcus had somehow put up a table and spread out lunch without my noticing.

"Food is important," Sill said.

As we settled into our chairs, DeMarcus led another man toward us. He was a tall man, with a military posture, I thought. I might have thought that even if he hadn't been wearing an army uniform.

"Hello, General," Sill said.

"John." He shook Sill's hand.

"General Takitall, I'd like you to meet my new associates, Professors Eigen Vector and Wala Kitu."

"Please, call me Auric," the general said. He looked at me. "Professor Kitu, I've heard so much about you."

I was surprised but did not show it. "General."

"Sit, Auric. Have some lunch," Sill said.

On the table was a platter covered with Almas caviar, the dark, greenish-black roe surrounded by thin slices of Densuke watermelon, the black rinds beautiful against the red flesh. My eyes stopped at the platter right in front of me.

"Is that . . ."

"Yes, fugu," Sill said. "If that is what you were thinking. I have a fugu chef in the kitchen. It's a frequent treat."

"Fugu?" Eigen asked.

"Yes, puffer fish," John said. "Deadly toxic if not handled with the utmost precision. Every bite is an adventure. Please, try it."

"That's why I don't eat it," Takitall said. "I never know when I've outlived my usefulness with this one."

Sill and Takitall laughed.

I took one of the translucent slices and put it on my plate. I placed a bit of the raw fish on my tongue and let it melt.

"Heavenly, isn't it?" Sill said. "Don't forget the dessert. Those are real Famous Amos cookies."

"At least something here is rare," I said.

"I don't think Wally would like to hear that," Sill said.

"Excuse me," I said.

"Wally Amos bakes these every morning. He lives in one of the guest cottages."

"The real Famous Amos," I said. For the first time I felt myself in awe and found the feeling slightly embarrassing.

"Soon we'll all be as famous as Amos," Sill said. He and Takitall laughed again.

Eigen looked at me, wanting to laugh, but sharing my confusion.

"I'm sorry, I'm sorry," Sill said. He put his hand on Eigen's arm. "Auric, General Takitall, is the commanding officer at Fort Knox."

"General Auric B. Takitall, commanding officer of the US Army Human Resources Command, Fort Knox, Kentucky, at your service," Takitall said, saluting, clearly not taking himself seriously at all. "I love that shit."

"At your service," Sill repeated. He saluted as well. "DeMarcus!"

DeMarcus was there as if he already had been there. "Sir?"

"Bring the general his drink," Sill said.

"It's so early," Takitall said.

"What do you military types say? The White ones, I mean."

Takitall laughed. "It's five o'clock somewhere. Vodka and ginger ale."

"Very good, sir." DeMarcus remained, waiting.

"To drink?" Sill asked me.

"Nothing, thanks."

"Eigen?"

"I'll try the vodka and ginger ale," she said.

"Have you ever had alcohol?" I asked Eigen.

She shook her head.

"Fuddy-duddy," Sill called me. "DeMarcus, bring Eigen a weak one. And I'll have my usual."

DeMarcus nodded and walked away.

Takitall watched the servant leave. "Can he be trusted?"

"DeMarcus?" Sill laughed. "He's like a member of the family."

"Still, he's White."

"I'm White," Eigen said.

"But you're a mathematician," Sill said. "You're not quite of this world. Like Wala, here. He's, well, he's nothing. Right, Wala?"

"Nothing," I repeated.

"Yes, you're the nothing man," Takitall said to me. "Do you really believe in nothing?"

"I do."

"It's that powerful?"

"Like nothing you've seen. Or rather haven't seen."

Takitall smiled, nodded.

"So, Auric, is everything in place?" Sill asked.

DeMarcus, suddenly there again, set down the drinks. "And your Angostura Legacy, sir. Chilled to 0.55 degrees Celsius, as you like it."

Sill stared at his glass, the golden color of the liquid. "Yum, rum."

DeMarcus walked away.

"You were saying," Sill said to the general.

"Damn near ready." The general looked at all of us in turn. "Lady, gentlemen, as we say in the military, we're going to do *something*, even if it's wrong."

"And especially because it *is* wrong." Sill raised his glass.

4

Back on my veranda I coaxed Trigo into making a poop. Just as I had wiped his bottom there was a knock at my door. I opened up to find DeMarcus there.

"Yes?" I said.

"The poop, sir. I'll take Master Trigo's excrement."

"How did you know?"

"It's my job, sir." He had a plastic bag with him.

"I usually just flush his shit away like my own."

"How reasonable," he said. He put the bag in his pocket. "Will there be anything else?"

"Yes, would you call me Wala?"

"I'm afraid the master wouldn't like that."

"Very well. Then, I'll address you formally to keep things equal. What's your last name? The name after DeMarcus."

"There is none."

"So, it's just DeMarcus. Like Cher."

"Quite so, sir."

"Okay, then. I don't need anything else."

"Yes, sir."

I returned to the veranda and sat with Trigo. My friend looked at me and wanted to speak. I understood him all too well. He wanted to say, "Darwin was right. A mathematician is a blind man in a dark room looking for a black cat that isn't there."

"How true," I said.

Trigo rolled and exposed his round belly for a bit of scratching.

"Does that feel good, buddy?" I asked.

"Here's one. A mathematician is asked if he'd rather have cold coffee or meet God. He says he'll have the cold coffee."

"Why does he say that?" I asked.

"He's been told that nothing is better than meeting God and cold coffee is better than nothing."

"Wala, wake up." It was Sill. The sky was dark. I was still on the veranda. "Time to get up."

"Is it dinnertime?" I asked.

"No, we don't eat dinner around here. Want to see something cool?"

"Who doesn't want to see something cool."

He didn't seem to mind my sarcasm. "Let's go."

I followed Sill down the corridor, but he stopped shy of the stairs and turned into a room that I might have guessed was a closet. Inside there was in fact a wall of shelves cluttered with cleaning supplies. On the opposite wall was a huge five-foot-square map of Miami. He closed the door and we stood there.

"And?" I said. At that moment I felt the floor drop. We did also drop, as the room turned out to be a rather speedy elevator. We descended many meters in a short time. My first thought was how and when I would get back up to Trigo. The machine stopped and all was momentarily silent.

Sill opened the door. We stepped into a cavernous room, brightly lighted from above. The pings and bells and whirs of machines filled the air. There was an array of ductwork and above that a grid of shining steel catwalks. There were men and women dressed in sky-blue lab coats. It was the smell of seawater that drew my focus to the central feature of the cave. This was a submarine bay and parked in the center of it was in fact a submarine, but not like any picture of a sub I had ever seen. It was sleek, perhaps twenty meters long, with a squat conning tower that did not taper like a normal sail. Instead of sail planes, flat fins encircled the tower and the hull of the boat and so it looked like a kielbasa wearing a flared skirt.

"Nice sub," I said. "Did you buy or is it a lease?"

"Built it." He wiggled his fingers in the air. "Isn't she beautiful? I have no idea why boats are always female, but so be it. Even the USS *Abraham Lincoln* is a she. I thought of calling this boat the *Mary Todd*, but she was crazy and *tod* means dead in German, so you can see that wasn't going to fly. Or swim."

"Why do you have a submarine?"

"I'm a supervillain."

"I forgot." I looked around. The staff, the crew, the technicians, whatever they were, all young, Black, and beautiful, moved from machine to machine, from terminal to terminal with deliberation and focus. "Where is Eigen?"

"She was tired after her tennis lesson. Tennis is an exhausting pastime. Went right to sleep."

"Really?"

"No, I drugged her."

"What?" I asked.

"Well, you know, she kind of follows me around. Piaget and all that. She's cute and everything, but her non sequiturs are killing me. You're a little bit tedious on that front as well, I'll have you know."

"She's a genius," I said. I felt I had to say it.

"Jesus, Wala, I know that. That's why she's here. But the non sequiturs." He blew a breath of frustration through his lips. "We were having sex this morning and do you know what she said?"

"Oh my God?"

"I wish. No, she said, 'If I were wearing shoes right now, do you think they would match?' Then she screamed, 'Assume x is a Kähler manifold.' That was her orgasm, if you can believe it. Now, don't get me wrong, that's pretty hot, but hell, I don't even know what that means."

"Hodge conjecture," I said. "It states that certain de Rham cohomology classes are algebraic."

"Shut up." Sill folded a stick of gum into his mouth. "Want one?" I shook my head no. "Come on, nothing man, come see what the latest in superfast submarine technology looks like."

"I'm not an engineer," I told him.

"I know that. You're as bad as Eigen. What do you say when you orgasm?"

"I wouldn't know."

"That was a rhetorical question, but that was quite an answer. Very telling. A bit disturbing."

I thought he was making fun of me.

The boat was nothing like the *Nautilus* of Jules Verne I had imagined in my brief childhood. In fact, once we were down the ladder from the conning tower, there was very little seafaring-looking about the bridge. Three crew members sat on ergonomic chairs at sleek Lucite desks. A large transparent display in the center of the room showed a nautical chart of Biscayne Bay. Monitors lined the walls, flashing graphs and charts.

"Looks like an insurance office," I said.

"Really?" Sill sounded disappointed.

"Well, it doesn't much look like *Das Boot* or *Run Silent, Run Deep* or *The Enemy Below* or even *Hunt for Red October*."

"I get it. Everyone's a critic. Would you have me hang hams and large cheese wheels from the pipes?"

"I guess not," I said as I looked at the ceiling and saw no pipes, no valves, levers, or wheels.

Sill clapped his hands. "Where are my manners? Everyone, this is Professor Wala Kitu. He'll be with us for this little outing, perhaps for a while. I'll have you know he's a genius. I don't know if you can tell by looking at him, but he is. He's not a snappy dresser, but he is a fucking genius."

The crew nodded hello.

"How deep will it go?" I asked.

"Not *it*, *she*."

"Sorry."

"Two hundred meters."

That information didn't mean anything to me. I was simply trying to make conversation. "And how fast will *she* go?"

"That's the fun part. This boat can achieve seventy-five knots submerged."

I stared at him. "That's almost ninety miles per hour."

"Eighty-six and change," Sill said. "Do you find that hard to believe? So does the DEA. I like to take the girl out just to fuck with them and the Coast Guard. Shall we?" Sill didn't wait for an answer. "Make ready the boat," he said.

The crew at their desks, two woman and one man, to be precise, didn't seem to do much. The order was repeated by a woman with an enormous afro. They pushed a couple of buttons, the monitors changed, a few electronic tones rang out. Sill sat in a throne-ish chair midroom and sank into it. I could see that he was driving the boat with a stick, not unlike the joystick of an old airplane.

I stood beside him. "I assume there are other crew about the boat."

"Yes."

The vessel rocked gently. It was a nice feeling.

"Dive the boat," Sill said. He looked at me. "I love saying that."

Again the order was repeated by the same woman. She caught me looking at her and smiled.

"Make our depth twenty-five meters. Make heading one-eight-zero. Ahead one-third." Sill beamed.

The woman with the afro repeated the orders without taking her eyes from mine. I looked away. I looked at the screen in front of Sill, which showed a forward view of our movement.

"We'll clear the bay and open her up," Sill said. "Then the fun starts. Would you like something? A cookie, some water, milk? Tea? Is the coffee made?"

"Coffee is brewing," a young man said.

"A cookie would be nice," I said.

"Cookies for everyone."

"Right away, sir." DeMarcus startled me and I jumped. I hadn't noticed his presence or his arrival. He left the bridge, passing through a bulkhead door.

"He's amazing, isn't he?" Sill said.

"He's a ghost," I said, nodding in agreement even though Sill was not looking at me. The bridge crew acted as if they were in a business office in downtown Providence rather than under the sea. They applauded when DeMarcus returned with an assortment of cookies on a large platter.

"DaMarcus's sugar cookies are especially good," Sill told me. "And much enjoyed by the crew."

"Thank you, sir," DeMarcus said. "Will that be all?"

Sill gave a dismissive wave and DeMarcus was again gone.

"So, what are we doing out here?" I asked.

"Gloria, what kind of activity do we have on the surface?" Sill looked to the woman with the afro.

Gloria took a bite of chocolate chip cookie. "Five or six cruise ships, the usual smattering of smudges."

"That's what we call anything less than ten meters," Sill said.

"More yachts than usual," Gloria continued. "Gates's boat is up there. In her usual spot."

"Ostentatious bastard," Sill muttered. "Do-gooder."

"And what have we here?" Gloria said. She finished her cookie. "The signature reads as a Sentinel-class cutter." She looked at her screen. "One hundred fifty-four feet long, a fast-response patrol boat."

"That wasn't here last week," Sill said.

"Nope," said Gloria.

Sill looked at me. "Last time we were out, they had some hulking tub that looked like the *Minnow*."

"The *Minnow*?" I asked.

"I forgot who I was dealing with." He turned back to his crew. "Do they know we're here?"

"I don't think so," a bespectacled man said.

"Well, alert them to our presence. Give a ping."

"One ping," the man said and that cliché sound of every submarine film I had ever seen sounded. "That got their attention."

"How far out?"

"Six hundred meters and closing," Gloria said. "Bearing one-zero-five."

"What's the top speed of that thing?"

She looked at her screen. "Twenty-eight knots."

"Make speed twenty-eight knots," Sill said. "Let's allow her to chase us for a while. We'll head up into the bay and make her dodge some smudge, then pop out like we're headed to Cuba."

"Why are we doing this?" I asked.

"Because, Mr. Bond, we can." Sill and the crew laughed.

5

When we arrived back at the submarine bay, I had the brief and unsettling thought that perhaps none of any of that journey was real, that it was all faked. We could have been sitting right where we were now, docked, the boat, if it was that and not a prop, rocking on the water. All on a soundstage. There were no windows through which to see out. The screens were all simply screens and could show anything one wanted. I didn't, at any time, feel the least bit motion sick, but I never had before anyway and, for all I knew, submarine travel perhaps didn't make anybody feel nauseated. But why would he fake such a thing? Certainly not for my benefit. The bridge crew exited the boat with us. Gloria and I shared eye contact as we walked separate ways, she toward what looked like a lab of some kind and I, stepping in Sill's tracks, back to the elevator that had brought us down. We said nothing in the moving room until it stopped.

"Thank you?" I said.

"Wala, I know this is a lot to take in," Sill said. "I mean, you've been here only one day."

"Do you believe you're under surveillance?" I asked.

"I most certainly am. I have the house electronically swept every other day. It takes them at least a day to realize that their devices have been.neutralized." He led the way toward the library. "The thing about being a supervillain is that everyone knows about you. That's sort of what makes it fun. See that painting?" He pointed to a wall in a sitting room.

"The copy of the *Mona Lisa*?"

"Not a copy. I stole that some five years ago. It's an unreported theft because it's so embarrassing for the museum. I stole it in broad daylight. It's worth more to the Louvre to let me keep it and have everyone believe that such a crime is unimaginable than to possess the real thing. Hell, no one is ever close enough to it to see the difference. What, is some Austrian businessman going to start shouting that it's a fake? So, better to accept the loss."

"That's crazy," I said.

"I suppose. But true nonetheless. If three million eager tourists learned that they had crowded together in that room last year to get a distant glimpse of a fake, what do you think would happen? It would call into question the authenticity of every work in the museum. Can I sell it? No. I don't need to sell it. You know what, if you get really close and stare at it for a while, you won't be so impressed. Don't get me wrong, it's a work of genius. Marketing genius."

"Back to your seafaring activities. What does any of this have to do with Fort Knox?" We stepped into the library and immediately I felt more relaxed. "You can't very well sail that thing to Kentucky."

"First of all, you don't sail a submarine, but you know that. Can't a man have hobbies? Even a diabolical fiend, such as myself, has to blow off a little steam now and again. Villainy is tough work."

For some reason my mind turned to Eigen. "Should you check on Eigen? After all, you drugged her."

"She's fine. Just a little gamma-hydroxybutyric acid."

"I'm afraid that means nothing to me."

"Liquid ecstasy. Though I have to admit with her constitution a glass of champagne would have sufficed."

"What is your favorite book in here?" I asked, changing the subject.

"You might think it would be my Gutenberg Bible. There are only forty or so of them left and this one is actually the very first one off the press. But it's not. It's this Gutenberg, *Ars minor* by Aelius Donatus. I can't read a word of Latin and I don't know who the fuck he was, but this is the first book Gutenberg printed."

"Stolen?" I asked.

"Of course. I'm a thief, Wala. I stole this from a Russian military base. It had been in a Soviet armory, but it had become home to the Russkiy Voynneyy Dzhaz-bend, pardon my bad Russian. The Russian Military Jazz Band, the official name. They specialized in Gershwin and Goodman."

"Why was it there?" I asked.

"The Russians stole it from the Germans at the end of the war and, like most things, forgot where it was, what it was, or that they even had it."

"Why do you love it if you can't read it?"

"I love it *because* I can't read it. It could say anything."

"But it doesn't," I said. "The title means small art. May I see it?"

Sill opened a drawer under the Gutenberg Bible and lifted a small book with great care. "Here it is." He handed it to me. "It's a little fragile."

"I should think so." I took it from him, opened it, turned a couple of pages. "This is a textbook, a grammar book."

"Oh." Sill sounded disappointed. "You've ruined it for me."

"Sorry, but isn't it better to know?"

"I'll get back to you on that." He looked out the big window at the bay. "You should probably see to your dog."

I went back to my room to check on Trigo but opened the door to find Eigen lying on my bed, her face mere inches from the dog's face. "Fat face," she said. She was still dressed as if playing tennis.

"How are you?" I asked.

"He pooped," she said.

"That's good. How was your lesson?"

"To tell the truth I don't really remember the lesson."

"Do you have a headache?" I asked.

"As a matter of fact." She still lay on her side, her eyes on Trigo.

"Try rubbing your temples with your fingertips." I showed her what I meant. "It helps when I have a headache."

"Do you believe that animals can talk?" she asked.

"I do."

"Has Trigo ever talked?"

"Let me get you some water," I said. "That sometimes helps, too." Before I could move toward the bathroom there was a knock. I opened the door to find DeMarcus with a tray on which sat a pitcher of water, two glasses, and several choices of pain medication. I took the tray from him and put it down. I poured a glass.

Eigen sat up and took the glass with both hands, looked at the surface of the water. "I feel like the molecules on the surface of this liquid," she said. She touched the water with the tip of her finger. "Underneath, the molecules can spread out equally in all directions, but on top, the molecules have to pull inward into the water, unable to press upward into the world. That's how I feel, like I'm contracting to a minimum surface area."

I nodded. "Do you remember anything? Did anyone hurt you?"

"Why would you ask that?"

I paused. "Because of what you just said about surface tension."

"Oh." She dipped her tongue into the water, paused, and then drank all of it. "I'm supposed to teach tomorrow."

"I don't know if that's going to happen. But maybe Sill will fly you home in the morning, if you ask. What happened to wanting to be bad?"

It was as if I had reminded her of some truth. "That's right. You're right. Bad. God, I'm so stupid. I wish I was more like you."

"How is that?"

"Brilliant, like you."

"Eigen, I didn't talk until I was five."

"You couldn't speak?" she asked.

"I *wouldn't* speak. At least, I assume I could have if I had chosen to. What I did choose to do was write notes and that only got me into trouble. I was loose with my notes. I learned that it's best to keep most ideas to oneself."

"I talk too much," she said.

"It's late, Eigen."

"May I sleep here?" she asked.

"Why?"

"I'm scared."

I said okay and she handed me the empty glass, lay back down, and pushed her nose into Trigo's. "Fat face. I love this face."

"I'll sleep out on the veranda," I said, but I was not certain she heard me. Trigo seemed happy and so I left him where he was.

6

I was asleep, uncomfortable and in a dream. I understood in my dream that I was nowhere but in my head. The Mount Rushmore in front of me was not in South Dakota and the mile-wide gorge behind me was not in Arizona, but in the space I had constructed. Trigo had all four legs, and though they appeared to be functional, he refused to either stand or walk on them and so I carried him. For some dream reason he had an English accent, not a posh James Mason sort, but one with corners, like the actor Michael Caine's.

"How long have we know each other?" Trigo asked.

"Five years."

"My, but doesn't time fly? *Mal fliegt.* Do you know how difficult it is to affect an English accent while speaking German? Seems like only yesterday I was lying there in that cardboard box on the sidewalk outside the Euler-Fermat Center for Formerly Exceptional Children Who Grew Up to Be Socially Awkward Adults, the EFCFECWGUBSAA. You were on your way to receive an award for managing to avoid suicide, if not suicidal thoughts, for thirty-five years of life, but you never made it in there. Instead you paid five dollars to the dirty, dreadlocked White boy who claimed I was the only survivor of a litter from a bitch that died giving birth."

"What are you talking about?" I said. "I found you at the

Providence, Rhode Island, Society for the Prevention of Cruelty to Animals, the PRISPCA."

"Don't be an asshole."

We moved along the rim of the canyon, what I took to be the south rim, but it was the north side. I considered my feelings, not an activity that often entertained. To designate feelings, to verbalize them, was to, necessarily, alter them, with no particular direction or mission. When I was very young, I didn't trust speech, believing that other, nonword languages would intrude, complicate, or obstruct meaning, body language, facial expressions, timing, inflection, and so I wrote notes, letters. Now I knew that any movement from initial, pure thought was a movement away from precise meaning or representation. What Trigo had taught me was that pure meaning did not exist, never did and never would. Meaning is always constructed after the fact. Not only is there no private language, but there is no such thing as private meaning.

"I know what you're thinking," Trigo said.

"Very funny," I said.

"Any idea, feeling, experience that moves from thought to utterance and tells you it is true is a lie," the dog said, all Michael Cainey. "Conversely, any utterance, written or spoken, that professes to be false, is true."

"And why are we having this conversation?" I asked.

"For the sake of negation."

"You mean it all means nothing," I said.

"Nothing."

The sun pounded down on us and a bunch of dreamlike things danced about, the world asserted its form, its dreaminess. But I expected as much from my dreams. My dreams, like the world, being made up, as it were, of unexpressed facts, unuttered observations, unformalized logical statements, remained pure and true and yet without meaning, until nullified by utterance. Isn't anything sacred? Nothing. Nothing is scared.

The sun did not grow hotter, but I did, hotter and hotter until I fell awake to find Eigen lying on top of me in the lounge chair on the veranda. She smacked her lips and breathed her awful morning breath in my face. Beside me was a cart that had not been there when I settled in for the night and on it was a full breakfast for two. It had no doubt been stealthily delivered by the ghost, DeMarcus. I remained still, not because I thought Eigen needed rest, not because I enjoyed her body pressed against me, but because when she awoke she would no doubt talk and whether she would expect me to talk as well didn't matter, as I simply did not want to listen. Trigo was asleep at my side in the chair, snoring, twitching.

I looked out at the bay and saw a Coast Guard cutter cruise south toward the sea on the Miami Beach side of the island. I imagined it was the same vessel that Sill had claimed to toy with the day before.

Eigen opened her eyes and brought me into focus. "Fat face," she said. I didn't know if she was talking to me or Trigo. I then saw that her hand was stroking the dog. "Do my shoes match?"

I looked down to see her bare feet again, realizing as I did that all of her was bare. "You're wearing no shoes," I said.

"So, yes," she said.

"They also match what you're wearing."

She looked at herself. "So they do." She closed her eyes and sighed. "Is this awkward?"

"Probably only to other people," I said. She and I were always awkward; it was our usual status or posture in the world, and so acceding to it, recognizing it of course served to neutralize it, if not negate it.

"How did you sleep?"

"Apparently on my side and naked," she said.

"What do you want to do?"

"What do you mean?"

"Go back to Providence and unpack Fermat's last theorem for some privileged young people or stay here and be bad?"

"I don't know." She sat up. "Look at the food."

"Yes. DeMarcus."

"Do you suppose he saw me naked?"

"It's very likely. Does it matter?"

She shrugged and popped a grape into her mouth. "It's pretty here. I might like to stay."

Trigo woke up, barked to tell me.

"Trigo has to poop."

"I should get dressed and go to my room."

"Okay."

Eigen stood, stretched, bare and unabashed. "I don't think he'll let me go back now," she said.

"Why do you think that?"

"I think I heard him talking to someone. Anyway, I have a memory, I think, of hearing him talking to somebody. Or it was a dream. I don't know. He said something about things starting to get rolling, that the window is open, the stage is set, the ducks are lining up, the storm is gathering."

"That's what you heard?"

"Does sound more like a dream, doesn't it?"

I put some bacon into Trigo's mouth. "Sill has a submarine. Did you know that? It looks like a spaceship. Do you think he's dangerous?"

"Oh, yes," she said.

Corsica

1

After receiving a new set of clean clothing from DeMarcus, quite remarkably identical to my dirty clothes, down to the striped tie I used for a belt, I found myself again on Sill's fancy jet flying away from Miami. I, reluctantly, but confidently, left Trigo with DeMarcus. He seemed absolutely unfazed by the instructions regarding my one-legged friend's bodily functions. And I liked him, DeMarcus. His lack of affect came across to me as trustworthiness and dependable. Sill was coy about our destination, said only that it was an island and that we would love it.

"I don't know why we have to fly way up to Iceland to get across this damn ocean," Sill said. "But that's what my pilot tells me."

"The curved route is shorter than the straight one," I said.

"What?"

"Euclid doesn't work on Earth," Eigen said. "Only in space."

"You see, this is why I have you two with me. Well, it's a long flight, regardless. There are snacks and drinks in the back. I am quite fond of snacks. Luckily I have a fast metabolism or else I'd be fat."

Perhaps Sill had drugged me the way he had Eigen or perhaps his expensive jet was just so insanely comfortable, but whatever the cause I found myself drifting into a deep, luxurious sleep. Trigo was not with me so I did not dream.

We landed very briefly at a private airport in Scotland. I was told it was Scotland and by the fog I was certain that was true.

"I don't have my passport," I said.

"Me, either," Eigen said. "If fact, mine is expired, having never been used."

Sill unwrapped a chocolate candy bar, stared at us, and took a big bite. "Fuck passports," he said. "We don't need no stinkin' passports. *Treasure of the Sierra Madre*. You ever see it? No? Jesus."

Despite the fog we somehow managed to get airborne again and again I was asleep.

I awoke to see Sill waking Eigen with a gentle kiss on the forehead. I looked out the window and saw a small airport with no discernible marker. "Where are we?" I asked.

"Still on the plane?" Eigen said.

It was a mathematician's response. Of course she was correct, but the answer was useless. "And where is the plane?" I asked.

"We're in Corsica," Sill said. "Bastia."

We exited the plane and squeezed into a tiny Fiat sedan, drove away from the airport without even a glance from customs officers.

The coastal city was not terribly attractive. It appeared dingy and a bit run-down from the main highway early in the morning, but we were soon off that big road and driving east into the mountains. The hills were webbed with fog. The road was steep and twisty. I had exhausted my supply of sleep on the plane and so I stared at the back of Sill's head as we careened through one hairpin curve after another.

"Why are we here?" I asked.

"Preparations."

"That's cryptic," I said.

"We need rehearsals, practice. We need to operate as a single machine, a well-oiled machine, an organism."

"What is Fort Knox?" Eigen asked.

"Actually we have our sights set on the United States Bullion

Depository." Sill turned the car off the curvy road onto an even narrower one.

A couple of miles up into a dense forest we came to a guard station manned by men in uniforms that I didn't recognize. Red blouses and red trousers tucked into shiny black boots. The two men wore no hats but sported similar bowl haircuts. They raised the barrier to let us in without having to slow down. We came to a tall wall, perhaps twelve feet high and made of steel. Sill stopped the car and the massive gates slowly opened.

"Wow," Eigen said.

I thought it.

The gates opened and we rolled in. The world on the other side of the wall was not the same as that outside. It was a futuristic campus consisting of several sleek buildings of two or three levels, carved up by well-groomed pea-gravel paths for vehicles and pedestrians. Many crimson-uniformed men and women rode around in gold-colored golf carts or walked. Sill parked the Fiat.

We stood outside the car. Sill took a deep breath. "Welcome to the Complex."

2

In contrast to the opulent, lavish accommodations in Miami these were austere, spartan, but oddly no less comfortable, perhaps more a statement about me. Sill led me through white corridors and delivered me to the room that was all white, furniture, walls, tile floor, and there was conspicuously no art on any wall or surface. White clothes had been laid on the white bed covering for me with a note that said wearing them was not mandatory. Black ink on white paper, in a script that was almost childlike for its precision, but was certainly not the writing of a child, for its precision. The washroom as well was all white, down to the white unbranded tube of toothpaste and bottles of shampoos and lotions. My clothes felt dirty and uncomfortable after the long flight and so I showered and did change into the loose-fitting white linen trousers and short-sleeved white polo shirt. After slipping into the white boat shoes, I found the door to be locked. I sat on the bed and waited. I passed the time thinking about nothing.

My door finally moved and in stepped the afroed Gloria from the submarine, dressed in white like me. "How are you today, Professor Kitu?"

"Wala."

"Wala. I'm Gloria."

"I know," I said. "I'm fine. You got here fast."

"I got here as fast as you. I'm Mr. Sill's pilot."

"I see. And you're also a sonar operator on the submarine. What else do you do?" I asked.

She laughed. "Many things. I do many things. I see you've changed your clothes. Shall we go?"

"Where?"

"Lunch. As you know, Mr. Sill loves lunch. And this is an important one."

"How so?"

"John's associates, he calls them associates, from the different territories are here to make their quarterly reports. It's very serious business. I am told the stakes are extremely high."

"Gloria, are you a villain?" The words felt strange in my mouth.

"I suppose I am. I'm trying, at any rate. *Villain* is such an elastic, shall we say limber, term. One person's villain is another person's freedom fighter. I'm sure you've heard that cliché. Or something like it. Ready? Let's go." At the door, she turned to me. "We're having tater tots. I love tater tots."

Lunch was served at a long rectangular table with John Sill seated at the head. There was no one seated at the other end. I was placed next to Gloria as far from Sill as possible. To his immediate right was Eigen. Six men faced eight others on down the table. We were all dressed in the same white linen outfits.

"I love lunch," Sill said. "As always we're having the lobster frittata from Norma's in New York. Flown in this morning. And tater tots, the frozen kind, the cheap kind. They're the best. Don't you agree, Gloria?"

"Yes, Mr. Sill."

"Gentlemen, thanks to you as always for making the long journeys here to make your reports. I'd like to introduce our guests.

This White girl beside me is Eigen Vector. I'm having sex with her. And at the end of the table, next to Gloria, is Professor Wala Kitu. He'll be helping us with nothing. All aspects."

The men applauded. I looked at Eigen's face but nothing registered on it. In fact she wore a dim, mechanical, unchanging smile, unlike her own.

"Perhaps, Professor Kitu will speak to us a bit later about nothing." John then turned his attention to a doughy man seated across from me and three chairs closer to the head of the table.

"Agostinho Aguedo, our representative from western South America, would you care to share your report?"

Aguedo was visibly nervous, his white shirt showing sheer with perspiration, but then so were all the men. He closed his eyes briefly, fumbled with the stack of pages on the table in front of him, and stood. "Fellow villains, guests, Mr. Sill," he said. "The quarter ended positively, with prostitution taking an upswing. Our drugs sales held strong and steady. Graft and protection money saw a seven percent improvement and piracy, though newly controlled, yielded significant yield."

The men at the table nodded, but John Sill did not.

"We therefore ended up with a total eleven percent increase in net profits," Aguedo said.

"And yet that was three percent under your projected performance." Sill stood. "Under the projected," he repeated.

Aguedo was shaking.

"Sit down, Aguedo," Sill said, softly.

The man did. "Projections for the next quarter are much better. We're getting a handle on the piracy concerns and the new crop of girls is much prettier."

Sill looked at the ceiling and sighed. "I keep telling you that it's not about prettiness, it's about fantasy."

And then Aguedo was gone. He wasn't dismissed. He didn't get up and walk or run from the room. He dropped dramatically from view, as if the floor had opened and swallowed him. He and his chair were gone. The two men who had been his neighbors looked straight ahead, not at the spot that had been occupied by Aguedo.

The food arrived.

"Time to eat," Sill said, joy in his voice.

"Yum," Gloria said. "Tater tots."

"What happed to Aguedo?" I asked.

Gloria dragged her thumbnail across her throat. "No tater tots for him."

"You mean he's dead?" I tried to keep my voice down.

"Very much so," she said.

"Sill killed him?"

With admiration, devotion, adulation, love in her voice, between her thick, painted lips, in her almond-shaped brown eyes, in her poofy afro, she said, "He did." My awkwardness prevented me from feeling the full force of what I had just witnessed, but intellectually I understood the gravity of it all.

I located Eigen at the front of the table. Her smile was as it had been, hollow, dead, and doll-eyed. I knew I had to help my friend.

Sill stood and raised his glass. Everyone followed. He sang and the rest of the men fell in with him, with precise harmony and the whole barbershop bit.

We come from where we come from
We go to where we go
We kill those who get in our way
We kill for only show

We are villains in the morning
Bad guys in the night
We raise the evil demons
To combat the arms of right

We have brass monkeys in our pockets
Pistols in our vests
Bazookas in our trousers
And ice cubes in our chests

We steal when we are hungry
And even when we're not
We are that fabled frying pan
Talking to the pot

No one will ever beat us
Or get the upper hand
We are the sword of evil
Let loose upon the land

Hey!

Applause.

3

Gloria escorted me back to my quarters. I was confused when she walked inside with me. All the white, the floors, furniture, walls, our clothes, suddenly made me laugh.

"What's so funny?" she asked.

"So much white," I said.

"What?"

"Why?" I looked around the room, at my feet, at the soles of one of my shoes. "Where is the dirt?"

"John likes things clean."

"What will they do with the body?" I asked.

"Body?"

"Aguedo. Are they going to bury him? Cremate him? What do villains do with dead bodies?"

"Do you really want to know?"

I nodded.

"Sit down," she said.

I sat on the bed and Gloria sat beside me. She placed her hand on my thigh with a strange, gentle pressure. "Aguedo fell through the floor into what we call the shark pool. We call it that because it is a pool filled with sharks. Mako sharks, to be precise."

"And they ate him?"

"Well, no. The sharks are pretty well fed, but they like to tear things apart. I'm certain they ate some of him, but he pretty much drowned and will decompose in the pool. The catfish will eat him in time." She observed my face. "You asked."

"I suppose I did." I looked at Gloria's face. She looked suddenly younger. "What's your story? How did you get here?"

"What do you mean?"

I thought I had put forward a rather clear question, so I asked it again, slower. "How did you get here?"

"Sill found me at Caltech. I was there doing graduate study in geoscience, in particular working on the Chandler wobble. As you can imagine, I was bored to death. That's when Mr. Sill showed up and asked me if I thought I could manufacture an earthquake. You have to admit that's an intriguing question."

"That's one way of seeing it," I said. "What did you tell him?"

"That is when Mr. Sill showed up and asked me if I thought I could manufacture an earthquake."

"I heard you."

"I said I didn't think I could and he asked if I wanted a more exciting career. I said yes and here I am."

"Before that?" I asked.

Gloria sighed and seemed to relax into herself, as if relieved to have that question. "I grew up in New York. My father was a hard-working man. He worked in a dry cleaners for years and saved enough money to finally buy the store. He opened a second store by the time I was eight. Then another. He did really well. And we moved on up, to the east side, to a deluxe apartment in the sky. Yes, we moved on up. We finally got a piece of the pie."

"That sounds like a familiar story," I said.

"Those were good times," she said. "I miss my two brothers. My older brother was an artist. He was shot by a Chicago policeman for standing around being Black."

"I'm sorry."

"He used to paint these elongated people like El Greco." She smiled, shook her head. "And my baby brother. I don't know where he is now. He was a real little talker, that guy. He really gave my parents a run for their money. My father called him the militant midget."

I stared at her.

"Man, was it ever cold in Chicago."

"I thought you said you grew up in New York," I said.

Gloria cocked her head slightly. "No, Chicago."

"Did your family have a housekeeper?"

"Yes. No." She looked at me, then away, then at me again. "Those were good times. We were lucky to have them. Do you want to have sex?"

"No."

"Okay. Goodnight." She stood and walked out of the room.

I took off the white clothes and put on the white pajamas, which were fairly identical to the clothes I'd just removed, stretched out on the white bedcovers, and looked at the faraway white ceiling. I looked across the room at my dirty clothes, drab as they were, the only color in the chamber there except for me. I wondered if there were rooms identical to mine in the compound. I felt fairly certain there were. Then I wondered if I was in the same room I had been in before. If my dirty clothes had been placed on the identical dresser in another room, how would I know? I was lost in the building with no identifying markings on the doors and corridors. Would it matter? If I found out my room was a different one, would it have mattered?

Without Trigo there would be no dreaming, so I tried to entertain myself before drifting off into my dead sleep. The ship of Theseus came to me, a problem that had amused me as a child. Heraclitus, for all his fragments, solved nothing with his puddle jumping. Replace the masts, the hull, the rudder, the sails, every sheet and board and is it Theseus's ship? Is it the same vessel only because it displaces water in the same spot? Is there a difference in replacing every piece of a thing in turn rather than replacing the whole thing at once? Eigen was occupying the space that she always had, but was she Eigen? If not, where was Eigen?

I had to find her.

I got up and went to the door and found it, to my surprise, unlocked.

4

Once in the hallway one thing was evident. If I didn't find a way to mark my door, I would never find my way back to it with any certainty. The soles of my shoes were clean, making it impossible for me to soil the white carpet outside my door. I had no pencil, no marker, and no blade with which to cut myself and so mark the door as if in Pharaoh's Egypt. I tried counting doors, but the corridor appeared endless, crossed as it was by many other corridors, white and all the same. How was Gloria able to find it?

A better, more pressing question was how was I going to locate Eigen? I did the only thing I could think of. I wandered the halls calling out, "Eigen, Eigen," like an idiot. Perhaps not even *like*, but *as* an idiot. Soon I was hopelessly, despairingly lost and puzzled all the more because none of the corridors led to anything that might have taken me out of the building. After coming to believe that I had covered the same hallways several times, never seeing a person or a color, I found myself standing in front of a vending machine. In it was nothing but bag after bag of barbecue potato chips. I had no change, no bills, no cards, as my clothes had no pockets. Though not hungry, I really wanted those chips, if only for the color. I shook the machine and startled myself with the noise and my own aggression. Then I shook it again, more vigorously, with equal success.

A door opened a couple of meters away.

"Wala?"

It was Eigen.

I ran to her door and pushed her back inside. Her room was just like the one I had lost. I looked around to see if we were alone. I glanced back into the corridor, found it still empty and white, or still, empty, and white, or still and empty white, then closed the door. Eigen was still dressed in white and her shoes were white, though both toes pointed the same way. I looked to see that there were many white shoes all over the floor, all white, lefts and rights, though she wore only lefts.

"Eigen, are you all right?"

"Look," she said, pointing down with her two index fingers. "My shoes really do match now."

I tried to get her to look at my eyes. "Do you know where we are?" I asked her. "Eigen?"

"A hotel? A hospital? Hospitals are often white like this. We're in a lab somewhere. Are we in a paint factory?"

I sat her on the bed. "Eigen, listen. Given any set A and any set B, x is a member of A if and only if x is a member of B, then . . ."

"A is equal to B," she said. "Zermelo-Fraenkel."

She was still in there.

"Wala?"

"Yes."

"Where are we?"

"Corsica."

"Where is Corsica?"

"It's in the Mediterranean, off the coast of Italy."

"We're in Italy?" she asked.

"Technically, France. We're in John Sill's compound."

"John," she said, her eyes again glazed over.

I grabbed her by her shoulders and shook her, remembering hearing that you're not supposed to shake babies and wondering if it was also true for mathematicians. I also found myself thinking in ways

I had never imagined, wondering, for instance, how an adversarial relationship with Sill might affect my returning to the US and, more importantly, to Trigo. Perhaps bringing Eigen out of her catalepsy was not such a good idea, at least not a timely one. I was concerned about her state, but if there were a change, might we go the way of Agostinho Aguedo, down a chute into the shark pool, so named because it was a pool filled with sharks?

"Wala," she said, sleepy seeming.

"It's okay. Just go to sleep, Eigen." I tipped her over on the bed and she did go right to sleep.

I walked out of her room and stood in the corridor. I had no idea where I was or where I was going or whether it even mattered. I knew only that the vending machine had not been near my quarters, so I walked away from it. I walked and walked, then decided to start trying knobs. If I encountered someone, so what? As it turned out, room after room was unlocked, room after room was ostensibly unoccupied. Twenty or so doors later, I decided that I would simply occupy a random room and did. I trusted that John Sill's people would find me.

It might have been morning when I awoke to knocking. I answered the door and there stood Gloria, dressed in a uniform reminiscent of an Italian street policeman, blue, complete with the white cross-body leather sash that held up a holster. There was, however, no pistol in the holster, but an old-fashioned slide rule. Of all the questions I could have asked, I, in fact, asked, "Do you know how to use the slide rule?"

"Why, yes," she said.

"How did you find me in this room?" I asked.

"What do you mean?" She seemed to lean toward me. "Mr. Sill likes that I can use the slide rule. It doesn't have a battery that can go dead. That's a wonderful feature, don't you think?"

"How did you know I was in this room?" I asked.

"I knew because you were not in any of the others."

"You checked them all," I stated, as a question.

"Of course not. Why would I check for you in a room you're not in?"

"But how did you know I wasn't in another?"

"Because you cannot be in two places at once. That would be physically and, especially, logically impossible."

"Again, how did you know I was in this room?"

She seemed to laugh or sigh. "Because if I had found you in another room you could not be here."

I didn't know which of us was Socrates and which was Dionysodorus. I let the matter go. "What time is it?"

"Seven-zero-three," she said without looking. "Time for breakfast. Rise and shine, Professor Kitu."

"Are we returning to Miami?" I asked. "Today, I mean."

"I don't know. Time for breakfast."

5

Breakfast was far more intimate than the previous day's late lunch. Sill's associates, confederates, accomplices were not there and so, aside from me, there was no candidate for the shark pool. For all I knew, they were all bathing in that special pool at that moment. The morning meal was served, thankfully, outside on a small tightly woven lawn, attended by Sill, Gloria, Eigen, and me. We ate omelets that Sill announced were made from gulls' eggs. They tasted just like chicken eggs to me and I said so.

"But they are gull eggs," he said.

"Why is that special?" I asked.

"Have you ever seen a gull's egg?" he asked.

I said I hadn't.

"Well, there you have it."

"While I'm asking questions," I said, "why are we here?"

"I had this meeting with the territories scheduled and, well, here we are. It's the kind of whimsical thing that we villains do from time to time."

It was difficult to argue with such reasoning. "Can we go back soon? I left my dog at your Miami house and though I believe DeMarcus is more than capable, I need to get back to him. And Eigen here has to teach next week."

Sill smiled. "We'll be on our way soon enough. We've got business in Tennessee coming, don't we? We can't forget that. That's why I hired you in the first place. Nothing will be coming to us very soon."

"About that," I said.

"Sorry, no returns."

"I haven't spent any of the money."

"You bought a car," he said.

"I did do that, but I can still give you back the full amount, all three million and whatever else you put in there."

"Good lawd, that's a lot of money," Gloria said with a strange and manic face.

"I don't think you understand, Wala. That money came out of my portfolio and as soon as it did it stopped earning. You would actually have to pay me back close to five million dollars."

"That's quite an increase," I said.

"What can I say, crime is a high-yield investment." He rubbed Eigen's thigh. "Right, my dear? I'm investing in you two. I do hope I've invested wisely. I sincerely hope that." He punctuated his words with a look into my eyes that might have been read as threatening or menacing by anyone who was not on the spectrum. But I am on the spectrum, and so I stared back at him.

"What are you thinking about, Wala?" he asked.

"Nothing," I said.

"Well, it's about time." He stood. "We would say *pack up*, but as there is nothing to be packed, I'll just say let's go."

"Where?" I asked.

"Miami," Sill said. "But first to a movie. It will be fun."

"A movie? I have no interest in seeing a movie. I just want to go home."

"It's a short movie." Sill looked at the sky. "We'll watch it and then, whoosh, off into the wild blue yonder. Besides, you haven't a choice. Everyone to the theater."

We walked across the compound (the campus, Sill called it) to what, even from the outside, looked like a theater. There was an old-fashioned ticket booth, at which Sill paused and pretended to purchase tickets from the dummy behind the glass. Inside there was a concession stand with real people behind the counter. There was an abundance of candies and we were instructed to just say what we wanted. "Your childhood favorites," Sill said. Eigen asked for Raisinets. I would have settled for a raison d'être, but it was not to be. I asked for Goobers. We four were the only audience in a room that must have sat three hundred people. We sat and the film started.

Un Chien Andalou. We watched and then the house lights came up. As we were walking out, Sill asked me if I was going to question him about his film choice. I said I was not. He nodded and smiled.

"Okay," I said, once outside. "Why a silent surrealist film that even Buñuel himself thought was shit?"

"You didn't like it," he said. "Eigen, did you like it?"

"They split open an eye," Eigen said. "I didn't like that. I didn't like that at all. Why did the man show her the time at the end?"

"He showed her his watch," Sill said. "You can't show time. Can you, Wala?"

"Were they dead at the end, buried in the sand like that?" Eigen was agitated. "Wala, were they dead? What did it mean? Wala?"

"Nothing," I said.

Sill gave me a friendly, warm, brotherly slap on the back. "We can go home now. Our chariot awaits."

The three of us, Sill, Eigen, and me, piled into a little Renault and drove back to the airport. I waved to Gloria. "Will Gloria take another car to the plane?" I asked. "I mean, she is your pilot, right?"

"Don't fret, Wala. Don't fret."

A bijective function

1

One might think that it would be hard for a one-legged bulldog to express emotion, but I can't tell you that is not true. Trigo was quite angry with me, as you say, pissed off. He seemed completely comfortable with DeMarcus, but he had a bone to pick with me.

"I'm sorry," I said to him.

He just looked at me and squeezed out a shit.

I apologized again and gave him a Goober off which I had sucked all the chocolate. He liked that. He softened. I put him in the Björn and walked to the library. I needed the comforting smell of old paper and hide glue. When I got there, I found a note on the case containing the Gutenberg Bible. It read: *Wala, figure out cardinality for me.* I was confused because I didn't know there was anything about cardinality to figure out. The number of elements in a set. What could be clearer? And because it was clear, the note troubled me no end. What was the cardinality problem? Could the note have been referring to the cardinality of the continuum or was it a reference to Hilbert's silly hotel, a thought experiment to which I responded that not only will there always be an infinite number of filled rooms, but an infinite number of empty ones as well? Was it a cryptic joke placed there by Sill to annoy and distract me or was it a cryptic cry for help from Eigen?

I looked out the window at the noon-lit Biscayne Bay. The Coast Guard cutter floated by. There seemed to be some kind of ceremony being held at the memorial on the tiny island in the middle.

Trigo perked up and suddenly DeMarcus was there.

"Lunch is served," the man said.

"Okay," I said. I felt the resignation in my voice.

"May I give Master Trigo a treat?" DeMarcus asked.

"Of course."

DeMarcus pulled a small can from his coat pocket. He pulled the tab and opened it. The smell of Vienna sausages hit me, familiar from my childhood. He reached in with his big fingers and extracted one, fed it to an eager Trigo. I thought I saw DeMarcus smile.

"He likes you," I said.

DeMarcus fed him another. "Is that too much?" he asked.

"I don't deny him anything," I said.

"Very good, sir." The can empty, it disappeared from view.

"Where is lunch this time?" I asked.

"Aboard the yacht."

"Of course."

I followed DeMarcus. Out at the dock I saw a sailboat that was perhaps nine or ten meters long. It was shockingly tasteful relative to all else I had seen, the jet, the helicopter, the submarine. My reaction must have shown on my face.

"I know," DeMarcus said.

I looked at him.

"Incongruous."

Sill, Eigen, and Gloria were already seated topside at an elegant table. Eigen was dressed in a red bikini, looking like a mathematician in a bikini. Gloria was dressed in white, as she had been in Corsica. Sill was comfortable in jeans and a Parliament (the band) T-shirt. That was when I realized that I was dressed very similarly to Sill and I didn't know how that had happened. I pulled my shirt away and stared at it upside down. Jethro Tull. I didn't know who he was, but he looked like an old man.

"On my second rum, old man," Sill said.

"Oh, Wala, isn't it a beautiful day?" Eigen said.

"Nice boat," I said.

"A seventy-nine Morgan," Sill said.

"I was expecting something grander," I said, meaning it as an insult.

"No doubt," he said. "It's unassuming and simple enough to drive the fucking feds crazy. As unassuming as a yacht can be. This is the sort of thing really rich people buy to show that they're rich enough not to need the crazy-ass expensive stuff that they keep at the other house. Like my jeans and T-shirt. Just looking at me you'd think casual dude, but if you knew that Bootsy Collins and George Clinton personally sewed the sleeves onto this bad boy, well, that makes it different, doesn't it?"

"I have no idea what you're talking about."

"Never mind. Sit." The Coast Guard cutter motored by. Sill waved. "Idiots. Captain McHale."

"Mr. Sill, I'd like to go back to Providence. Perhaps Gloria here will be kind enough to fly me up there." I nodded to Gloria and she nodded back, though it was none too clear that she knew at all what I was saying. "Eigen, don't you want to get back to your students?"

"Fuck 'em," Eigen said, in a voice far from her own.

"You don't mean that," I said.

"Of course I mean it. Why would I want to go back there to those privileged little bastards?" The was an undeniable edge to her voice, but her eyes, her gaze was as round as a basketball.

I sat down, looked across the table at Gloria. "Gloria tells me that you killed Aguedo. Is that true, that you dumped him into a pond of sharks?" After he nodded, I asked, "Just how many people have you killed?"

"Well, the sharks did the killing," he said.

"An important distinction," Gloria said.

Trigo barked.

"How many deaths are you responsible for?"

"You're such a fucking boy scout. And here I thought you didn't believe in anything," Sill said.

"No, I believe in nothing."

"I love it when you talk dirty," Sill said.

Gloria and Eigen laughed.

"Eat, eat, eat," Sill said. "Enjoy yourself. Gloria will fly you back to Providence after lunch and you can do whatever it is you do up there. Then you can make your way to Tennessee to meet me. Maybe drive your new car."

"Okay. I mean, okay about flying to Providence. Eigen, ready to get back to your classes?"

Sill sipped his rum. "Eigen will be remaining here."

"Eigen?" I tried to find her in her eyes. "Trigo would really like your company on the plane." I could almost hear her saying *fat face* but she didn't.

Instead, she stared at me for several seconds, then leaned back to let the sun strike her face.

2

Gloria drove me to the airport in a red '57 Ferrari 335 Spider. She took the curves with such mechanical, crackerjack adroitness that I felt no fear regarding our speed. We perhaps could have gone faster, but that would have required a different vehicle, as she had the Spider pushed to its limit. She didn't talk at all. I chalked this up to the fact that we would not have been able to hear each other over the roar of the twelve cylinders and the wind. Trigo seemed to enjoy the ride with his cheeks full of Miami freeway air.

When we had skidded to a stop, on the tarmac well inside the airport, at the door of the plane, Gloria finally looked at me and said, "Once on board, I will be in the cockpit, you will be in the cabin."

That sounded like a reasonable arrangement to me and in keeping with our paucity of conversation, I nodded. She followed me up and closed the door. And true to her word, she locked herself in the cockpit and left me with Trigo in the plushly appointed and well-stocked cabin. I buckled us in and in no time I was fast asleep.

Dream. Trigo had six legs and looked rather frightening. He moved around our kitchen at home like an insect, enjoying himself, looking at one paw and then another, but ignoring his left front.

"Where did you get all those?" I asked.

"The leg store," he said. "They were having a special."

"Why did you buy so many?" I asked.

"What do you mean?"

"I mean isn't four the standard number for a dog?"

"What do you mean standard number?" he asked.

"Dogs have four legs."

"I'm a dog and I had one leg. Are you saying I was supposed to have four?"

"Not at all."

"Well, I bought as many as would fit. They work nicely, I think. How do I look?" He pirouetted.

I couldn't help myself. "You're my best friend, so I have to tell you the truth. You look like an insect."

"Is that a bad thing?" he asked.

"Not if you're a beetle, but you're a dog."

"What are you saying?"

"Four is all you need."

"Actually three is all I need. I could learn to stand on two. Why isn't two all I need?"

"Most dogs have four."

"Most humans don't understand Euler's formula, but you do. So what are you saying? I think my legs look nice."

"I agree. So, what are you planning to do now that you've got them? And so many, I might add."

"Don't be an asshole. For one thing, I'm going to take you on walks so you don't get fat. And I might chase something."

"What would you like to chase?"

"Don't patronize me."

"No, I'm serious. What do you want to chase? Do you want to chase and catch or just chase?"

"I want to chase a pigeon, but I don't want to catch it. Disgusting creatures. Imagine having one of those in your mouth. Good Lord, the feathers."

"Trigo, are you worried about Eigen?"

"Yes."

"I think she's drugged," I said.

"At the very least. I can't believe we left her there."

"I know."

"What kind of a friend are you?"

"I know. By the way, I'm sorry I left you with DeMarcus."

"Are you kidding? I love that guy. Vienna sausages, salmon treats, belly rubs. If you didn't need me so much, I'd be with him in a second." Trigo beetled his way over to the window and looked outside. "Those FBI fellows are out there. Or whatever agency they're with."

"That's too bad." I looked at my feet. "Trigo, we have to save Eigen."

Trigo came back. "That's true. Eigen is proof of one thing."

"What's that?"

"There is in fact an odd number that is perfect."

I nodded.

"Professor Kitu. Professor Kitu."

"Trigo, why are you calling me that and why is your voice so strange?"

"Professor Kitu, wake up."

I opened my eyes and found Gloria's face very close to mine.

"We've landed," she said.

"We're in Providence?"

"Yes." She said only that. No eye contact. She walked away and I noticed that she was dressed in a pilot's uniform. She opened the door, then without a glance back reentered the cockpit and closed the door behind her. I put Trigo in his carrier and walked down the stairs to the tarmac.

From the private hangar it was a long stroll to the main terminal and the public buses. I realized during the walk that I was wearing no jacket, only jeans and the thin Jethro Tull T-shirt. It was freezing. I at least had a small source of heat strapped to my chest. I boarded the bus headed to town center and was greeted by a familiar driver, all three hundred pounds of him.

"What say, Prof?"

"Hi, Harold." I reached toward my pockets and realized they were empty, of not only money, but my wallet and passport as well. "I'm sorry, but I don't have any money" is what I said.

"Don't sweat it, Professor. I know you're good for it. Maybe Trigo has a few quarters." He scratched my friend's chin. "Right, Trig?"

"Thanks, Harold."

I sat in an empty row right behind Harold and looked out the window. The bus was heated and the blower was just above me.

"Where you coming from with no money or baggage?" Harold asked.

"Miami," I told him.

"That's why you ain't got no jacket."

"I suppose so," I said.

"So, were you lying on the beach living it up? What do they call it? South Beach? You stretched out on South Beach?"

"Not quite."

"Cheese stick?" Harold reached back, offering me one.

"Thanks." I unwrapped it. "Should you be eating these?"

"You mean because I'm big?"

"No, because you're fat, Harold."

"That's why I like you, Prof. You cut right through it. No bullshit with you." He turned the wheel. "My kid likes these in her lunch and so I always stick a couple in my pocket. Just a little cheese, right?"

I bit into the stick. "Just a little." I shared it with Trigo.

I got off the bus at the bottom of the hill and walked up toward my house. The air was much colder now and the wind picked up. The gray sky looked like snow. As soon as I had formed that thought, flakes began to fall.

3

True to his word, Sam had returned my car, parked it more neatly that I ever could have in the drive, and had passed the key through the mail slot in the door. The key was in a small envelope with a note that read: *Sometimes 2+2 is 4, at other times it only equals 4.* I liked the note and then tossed it in the waste can. My house no longer smelled of the gas that had been tossed in through the kitchen window.

I showered and changed into less exotic clothing, corduroy trousers and a blank T-shirt. Trigo barked in the living room, an angry bark. I walked one-shoed to find him pointing with his nose at Bill Clinton.

"If he had only one more leg he would kill you," I said.

"How was your trip?"

I looked around the room for anyone else. "Where is your partner? What's his name? Twitchell?"

"Mitchell. He's in the car listening to the radio."

I looked out the window. The snow was falling heavily now. I saw Mitchell there, sitting in the passenger seat. "What's he listening to?"

"I don't know. He loves country music. So, how was Miami?"

"You know about that, do you?" I picked up Trigo and sat on the sofa with him in my lap. "It was interesting."

"I can't impress upon you enough how dangerous John Sill is."

"I'm getting the picture," I said.

"Really? What happened?" Clinton asked. He sat on the stuffed chair not far from me. His attitude had changed. Now he was attempting to come off as friendly.

"What's the name of the agency you work for?"

"That's of no concern to you," he said.

"How do I know that you're not an operative of Sill's here to check up on me? Test my loyalty or ability to keep a secret or something like that?"

"Is there a secret?"

I looked him in the eye. "Yes," I said. "No," I said. "Maybe," I said. "There could be. There must be. I know there is one, but I don't know it. I don't know of one, so there couldn't be one. There might be a secret that which none more private can be conceived."

"You know, I don't like you," Clinton said.

"Good." I looked out the window again. "What is he listening to?"

"If I find out, will you tell me something that happened in Miami?"

"Sure, why not?"

Clinton pulled out his phone and called Mitchell, asked what he was listening to, said that he didn't need any help, just that he wanted to know what was on the radio. He hung up and looked at me.

"Well?" I asked.

"Patsy Cline. 'Crazy.'"

"Really," I said.

"That's what he said. Your turn."

"John Sill has a submarine," I said, flatly.

"That's something. What can you tell me about it?"

"It's wet."

"Does it figure into his plan?"

I leaned forward and he leaned forward to meet me. "What plan?"

"His scheme? Is he smuggling something into the country? Out of the country? You must know something."

"Three questions. I'm sure he is. I'm sure he is. And that is necessarily true, if you are a Cartesian, which I am certain you are." I stroked Trigo's back. "How did you know I was in Miami? Wait, let me guess, you guys put a microchip just under my skin while I was unconscious, and you're using global positioning to track my every move. Maybe in the back of my neck."

"Nice. But no. We're the government. We know where you are."

"About the microchip, you wouldn't tell me even if I was correct." Clinton shrugged.

I felt around the back of my neck and found nothing unusual.

"We know Sill is up to something. Just tell us what you know and all will be good in Mudville."

"What?"

"Tell me what you know."

"Nothing. I know nothing. I also know that Sill is up to nothing."

"You're telling me he's not planning anything."

"That's not what I said. Listen this time. Sill is interested in nothing. He wants nothing. He plans to take nothing. He wants, rather needs, me because I know nothing."

"Your colleague, Eigen Vector, what's her part in this?" he asked.

The question bothered me. I felt him notice that it bothered me.

"Touch a nerve?"

"I don't know why he wants her."

"What can you tell me about her?"

"Only that she's a brilliant topologist. That's it."

"You don't care that she might be in trouble," he stated as a question. "She's down there in Miami still, isn't she?"

I didn't respond. I thought about Eigen, being treated the way she was being treated. And then I thought of Gloria, who might have flirted with me initially, but it now seemed unlikely, as our interactions, including her offer of sex, were all so mechanical.

"Professor Kitu?"

"Yes."

"Yes, what?"

"Yes, I am worried about my friend."

"Why is that?" he asked.

I looked at his face and imagined it as two-dimensional and so saw right through him. "You are a strange man," I said.

Clinton stood. "All right, Professor. Just know that we're everywhere."

"I will rest comfortably knowing that," I said.

"You do that."

I looked out the window at Mitchell. "What's he listening to now?"

"Why do you care?"

"I'd just like to know."

Clinton pulled out his phone again. "He wants to know what you're listening to now. I don't know why. You come in and ask him. Just tell me." He hung up and looked at me. "Hank Williams, 'I'm So Lonesome I Could Cry.' What does that tell you?"

"Nothing."

4

It is not necessary that I address the notion of contingency, but I feel I have to. The question that has plagued me is not one of whether the world is fatalistic, I know that to be true, but rather, given that knowledge, how is it possible that some things are, in fact, contingent and, further, is the existence of contingency necessary? How else could we speak of necessary truth unless there was an opposite that allowed us the orientation from which to understand. Would we speak of night if it was always day? Could we? It was not until I was well into this mindless patter that I realized that I was asleep.

"Sleeping?" Trigo asked.

"Apparently," I said. "So, what do you think about what I was saying?"

"You mean that contingency shit?"

"Yes."

"That's the kind of thinking that becomes possible only with the closure of metaphysics. I mean you've exhausted all of your basic principles. I'll tell you what I think. First, forget the nonsense of this dream. It's no good for you, but it's all you've got. I think you should masturbate instead. It would be more honest. And cleaner."

"But what about our friend?"

"The one that calls me fat face?"

"Yes."

"She's sweet. I like her."

"What should I do?"

"She's kind of a ditz. Like you."

"Well, we're mathematicians."

"Excuses, excuses. You tell me. You're the one that moves around. You have a car now. Drive. Go get Eigen and bring her back."

A cell phone buzzed on the coffee table. Trigo and I looked at it. I didn't own a cell phone.

"Part of the dream?" I asked.

Trigo said nothing. I realized that I was awake.

"Hello?" I answered the phone.

"Wala, old boy, it's me, John. I need you to get in your car and drive to Washington, DC. Keep this phone with you. I'll give you further instructions when you arrive."

"Is Eigen with you?"

"Yes, here she is."

"Eigen?"

"Hi, Wala."

"Where are you?"

"I'm with John."

Another mathematician's response, true but useless.

"Are you in Washington?"

"We're on a train."

"Are you okay?"

"Where are you, Wala?"

"Providence."

"That's funny," she said. "I used to live there."

Sill came back to the phone. "DC. Leave now." He hung up.

I looked down at Trigo. "Let's pack a bag, boy. Looks like we have a long drive ahead of us." The snow was sticking and beginning to form a blanket on the yard. Had I good sense I would have felt some trepidation at the prospect of driving in such bad weather, given that my driving skills were virtually nonexistent, but I possessed no such sense.

I packed a bag. I then drove to the Goodwill store, where I purchased a child's car seat for Trigo.

For all y such that

1

I drove onto the road from the Goodwill parking lot without a mishap. I wondered whether that was the same as driving out with a hap. I could see that my route was exceedingly simple, one road, Interstate 95 all the way to Washington. I was not driving south because I had been instructed to drive south, though I had been, but because I, contrary to my nature, was concerned with the well-being of another. My lack of interest in the immediate and concrete future of any other human being was well known, and more evident to me even than others, so I was impressed by my action. Impressed in the way that I merely acknowledged a difference from my usual ways and conduct, though I didn't find my action, or pre-action, remarkable in any way. Though the drive contained many hair-raising moments, any one of which was certainly more exciting during than in the retelling, I will not suffer them now. I managed to negotiate my vehicle through hardly moving traffic from one side of New York City to the other, but in New Jersey I was pulled over by a highway patrolman. The blue-shirted, blue-capped officer approached cautiously, eyeing me through the side mirror, his hand resting on his pistol.

"Good evening, sir," he said. "Would you be kind enough to let me see your license and registration?"

He was very polite.

"I don't have either," I said.

"Say what?"

"I bought this car a couple of days ago. I do have the title."

"Driver's license?"

"No."

"Lost?"

"Never had one. Here's my passport. And my faculty ID."

"You don't have a driver's license."

I repeated, slowly. "I do not have a driver's license."

He looked back at the oncoming traffic, confused. "You telling me you have a car and no license."

"That is an accurate representation," I said.

"But you bought the car."

"Yes."

"Step out of the vehicle, please."

I got out and he turned me to face the rear door, pushed me into it. He kicked my feet apart and frisked me.

"Anything in your pockets I should know about?"

"No."

He looked in the back and saw the child's car seat. "Do you have a child in the car?"

"No, that's my dog."

He looked in. "What's wrong with him?"

"He has only one leg," I said.

"That's sad," the trooper said. "What's his name?"

"Trigo."

"Bulldog?"

"Yes."

"You know, you can't be out here driving with no license. This where you teach?" He waved my ID at me. "Brown University?"

"Yes. I live in Providence."

"Where are you going without a driver's license?"

"Washington."

He spoke into the radio on his epaulet. "I have a thirty-six-year-old Black male here, driving an '11 BMW with Rhode Island tags 7-1-6-6-5-5. Individual's name appears to be Wala, whiskey-alpha-Lima-alpha, Kitu, kilo-India-tango-uniform. About six feet, one sixty." He looked at me. "This all the ID you got? You realize of course that I have to take you in. You don't have a license."

"That's all I have," I said.

We waited for a few minutes. It felt like thirty, but was possibly two.

His radio sounded. "Ten-nine."

"Individual has no license. Name is Wala, whiskey—"

Radio: "Hold on."

Cars whizzed by. A light freezing drizzle began to fall.

"Eighteen?" from the radio.

"Go ahead," the trooper said.

"Does he have a dog with him?"

"What? Yeah. He's got a crippled dog in a baby seat. He's not armed. He *is* Black. You heard me say that, right?"

"Cut him loose," the radio voice crackled.

"He has no license. He's Black."

"Cut him loose, eighteen."

"Can you hear me clearly? I have a Black man here with no license driving a fucking BMW. He's got a faculty ID from some college in Rhode Island."

"Understood, eighteen. Now cut him loose."

The officer turned away from me, put his mouth against his device, and said, "He's Black. He really doesn't have a license."

"Let him go. Do you copy?"

"He's Black."

"Do you copy."

"Copy that." The trooper looked at me, but sort of through me. He was terribly confused and, indeed, so was I.

"Thank you, Mr. Kitu, you can go."

"Just like that?"

"I know, right?"

"May I ask you a question?"

He looked at me and nodded.

"Why did you pull me over?"

"You're Black."

"That's it? Because I'm Black?"

"That's usually enough." He looked south down the highway. "Your driving was a little erratic."

"That's because I learned to drive three days ago."

"What?"

"The woman I bought the car from took me to a mall parking lot and gave me a basic lesson."

He stared at me and walked away, on his radio again. "Base, I have to report that this guy doesn't even know how to drive."

"Eighteen, you have your orders."

"Problem?" I asked.

He turned back to me. "No. Go on, I guess. They told me to let you go. So go. Go before I shoot you."

I watched the trooper grow smaller in my mirror. It seemed odd that I would feel threatened by having been let go, but that was exactly how I felt. He had clearly received orders from someone other than his immediate superiors to let me go. But who? My money was on Bill Clinton, but I didn't really know whom he worked for. What troubled me was that they seemed to know where I was at any point in time and just where I was going. Perhaps there was a GPS tracker in my car or on me. Perhaps my apartment was bugged and they heard my conversation with Sill. Perhaps drones equipped with infrared cameras were flying through the dark above me at that very moment. I considered the possibility that Clinton and Mitchell were in a black midseventies Lincoln Town Car, following me at a prescribed distance, eating White Castle burgers out of a paper bag. My judiciously paranoid imagination was nothing if not excruciatingly detailed.

2

The night came on full and road matters went a little better for me after I managed to find the headlights and switch them on. The drizzle became a hard rain and the semitrucks roared past me, kicking up a spray that blinded me. I found the windscreen wipers and that helped some. I discovered that a small amount of pressure applied evenly and consistently to the accelerator made for a far more comfortable ride than pressing hard and releasing continuously. Seven hours later, at two in the morning, I was in Washington. Perhaps any city is dead at 2:00 a.m., but this city certainly was. I didn't know where in the city to go, so I drove and drove, past the White House, the Mall, up to the zoo, and back down into a deserted Georgetown. I parked and walked along a canal with Trigo on my chest.

I sat on a bench and looked at the cell phone that Sill had placed in my house. I suspected it would ring or chime or buzz at some point. I didn't know if Sill knew I was in Washington, didn't know if Clinton knew where I was. I was not completely certain I knew. Two men approached me. I stood.

"What are you doing on our bench?" the wider of the two asked.

"I was sitting," I said. "Now that I know it's yours, I'll be leaving it." I started to walk away, but the other man stepped in front of me.

"This is our sidewalk," he said.

"Wow, you guys must be rich," I said.

They looked at each other and the wide one said, "Oh, you got jokes."

"Give me your phone," the other said.

"I need it," I told him.

The wide one looked up and down the canal. "We need it more."

"I hardly think so," I said. "And how would one quantify and measure something abstract like need? I imagine it would be possible with something like food or medicine, but pencils, phones, or guitars, I don't know."

"I think there's something wrong with him," the narrow one said. "I'm pretty sure there's something wrong with him."

"I want your dog," the wide one said. "The phone and your dog and we won't beat the shit out of you."

I looked at them and tried to quantify as much as I could. The wide one seemed to be the leader. He was a couple of inches shorter than the other but had positioned himself slightly closer to me. His hands were relaxed and open while the other's left hand was clenched. He was standing on a slope, his stance narrow, his left foot about ten centimeters lower than his right, enough that his locked right knee had him listing about fifteen degrees.

"The phone and the dog," he repeated.

Trigo barked.

I recalled the anatomy books I had read. I pulled back my right foot and swung it with all my force toward the tibialis anterior muscle of his left leg. I sought to sink my toe deeply enough into his muscle that I might impress his peroneal nerve. He was duly impressed and he collapsed, rolled down the hill into the canal. The narrow one, now alone, backed away a step, reassessed me, then came forward again. His right hand was pulled back to strike me and so his left shoulder presented itself rather fully. With the knuckles of my right hand I struck him in his brachial plexus. His right hand detoured to cover his left shoulder and I kicked him in his mid right thigh, finding, it appeared, his sciatic nerve. He rolled down the hill, knocked his partner back into the water.

Trigo and I walked quickly back toward where I had parked.

"Impressive," someone said from the brush.

I stopped.

It was Sill. He was dressed in all black and I could hardly see him. "I had no idea you were capable of defending yourself," he said.

"Anatomy and physics," I said. "How did you find me?" I looked at the phone in my hand. "Of course."

The two men who had tried to rob me came trotting toward us. Sill stopped them with a raised open hand. "What kind of muscle are you two? You let a mathematician kick your asses?"

"Sorry, Mr. Sill," the wide one said.

"Go on back to the nest," Sill said.

"Yes, sir."

The two men trotted away.

"Where is Eigen?" I asked.

"Business first." He led me through the brush and to another trail. We were on yet another campus of some kind, it seemed.

"I believe I'm being followed or tracked," I said.

"Of course you are," he said. "What kind of badass villain would you be if you didn't warrant a tail."

"I'm no villain."

"But you are a badass."

"I wouldn't say that."

"I saw the way you took care of those guys. You're a badass, all right."

He stopped us at an old door in an old gray stone building. He used an ancient-looking key to let us in.

"Where are we?" I asked.

"This is the Naval Observatory."

"Why do you have a key?"

"Why not?" He led the way along a narrow corridor. "Wala, do you know anything about astronomy?"

"Only what I've read."

"How much have you read?"

"A couple of books," I told him. "Doesn't the vice president live here?"

"Yes. Near here."

"How are we able to move around like this?"

"It's the fucking vice president. Nobody gives a shit about him. He's the valet in arms, the official Ed McMahon. The Secret Service detail assigned to him are just mall cops with dark glasses."

"So what are we doing here?"

"Villain stuff." The corridor led to a wider hallway obviously meant for tourists. "The United States government has for years maintained an orbiter that passes for a simple commercial communications device."

"But it's not that," I said.

"Of course it's not that. Outside the range of normal orbits there is a craft that circles the planet and uses the innocent-looking device as a simple relay. It has a telescope as powerful as the Hubble, but it's not pointed at space. They call it a complex projective plane orbiter. COPPO."

"It's pointed at Earth."

"Of course. You know that expression 'If you can see them, they can see you'? Well, it ain't so, Bazooka Joe. That fucking telescope can spot a pimple on a Chihuahua's ass at night. If the president of South Korea opens her mouth, it can tell you if she has a cavity and how big it is."

"You're going to tell me something else about it."

"Clever man."

"Is it a weapon?"

"No." He paused, smiled, opened the door to the giant telescope room. "Not a weapon. Not exactly. I do have a rather expansive definition of the term *weapon*. It's not one in the conventional sense."

"What is it?"

"Wala, it's nothing. Absolutely nothing."

"You saying."

"Absolutely nothing."

The hairs on the back of my neck stood on end.

"Cool, right?"

"Why haven't any astronomers reported anything strange out there?" I asked. "It must have some kind of signature."

"Stealth technology maybe. Who knows. But it's there. And I plan to take it over."

"But if you can't see it . . ."

"I can't, you're right. But I know where it is."

"Where is Eigen?" I asked.

"Come, let me introduce you to someone."

3

At a computer terminal near the eyepiece of the giant telescope was a giant man. He stood to shake my hand upon being introduced, rising to his full seven feet. He smiled easily but was clearly nervous, if not shy. His name was Jean Luc Monfils.

"Jean Luc has been keeping up with the object for me," Sill said. "As I understand it, it's not an easy task. Some business about catching reflections of the signatures of other celestial bodies. Is that about right, Jean Luc?"

"Periodically, the craft appears, then disappears again," he said with a French accent. "It is read as an echo or sorts, clutter, sometimes space dust. That's why no one has discovered it or made note of it. Well, they have no doubt seen it and then thought, Oh that was nothing, or maybe said simply, That was weird. It's about to show up again. There is a distinct pattern." He pointed to a larger display with a laser pointer. "It will appear here, but just for a few seconds."

"*Dans la ceinture Kuiper,*" I said.

"*Très bon,*" Monfils said.

"*C'est là que je cacherais quelque chose,*" I said.

"Your French is good," Monfils said. "But you sound like an American speaking Parisian French. *Je viens d'Haïti.*"

"I have never been there."

"I don't like Parisians."

"I see."

"Now. There it is." Monfils pointed at the screen.

I tried hard to see what he was talking about. Sill was trying, too.

"Gone," Monfils said. "It was flickering, kind of greenish. Someone might think it was just a chromatic aberration, but we know better, don't we?"

"We do indeed," Sill said.

"Fourteen seconds. Not thirteen, not fifteen. Always fourteen."

"Next time it shows up, it's mine," Sill said.

"What are you talking about?" I asked.

"Two days, one hour, three minutes, and seven seconds," Monfils said.

"When that thing makes its next appearance, it will be vulnerable. That's when the comm satellite receives the data from the telescope, encrypts it, and sends it back to Earth as if it were just a bunch of calls to Grandma or Aunt Sally."

"Okay," I said. "So how do you end up with it? How does it become yours?"

"When that window is opened, so to speak, when that little lady up there cracks open her legs, to put it another way, I'm going to be there. I'm taking over and sending my instructions to it, ponying backward on the transmission it's streaming. Sort of like a digital salmon swimming upstream. Then nothing is mine. And we'll get to see just how much we can do with absolutely, positively, pure nothing. Excited?"

"I know I am," Monfils said.

"We had better clear out," Sill said. "The mall cops will be making their rounds soon. As you can imagine, it's rather difficult to conceal Monsieur Monfils."

"I'm tall," the astronomer said, putting on his leather-sleeved baseball jacket. "It's a liability in most situations."

The sun was just coming up when Sill took me into a nearly empty diner. We sat across from each other in a booth, leaned back against the vinyl while a sleepy, older waitress wiped down the table.

"You boys eating?" she asked. She took a step back when she realized there was a dog on my chest. "We don't allow pets in here."

"Yes, you do," Sill said to her. He handed her several hundred-dollar bills.

"Like I said, you boys eating?"

"Are we eating?" Sill asked me.

"Okay," I said.

"Coffee?"

"Yes, bring us some coffee," Sill said.

"I'll bring you some menus." The woman walked away.

"Where is Eigen?" I asked.

"She's in a room at the Four Seasons."

"What are you doing to her?"

"Why, whatever do you mean?"

"You're using her," I said.

"For what, Wala? What am I using her for?"

"I don't know."

The waitress delivered coffee and menus and left again.

"Sex," I said. "Maybe sex. Is it sex?"

"Would that bother you?"

"It doesn't bother me. I just want to know why you're interested in her. She's my friend and I don't want to see her hurt."

"Are you the big brother?"

The waitress came back.

Sill handed her both menus and smiled. "He'll have two eggs poached, bacon, and wheat toast. I'll have white toast."

The waitress looked at me as if for confirmation. I nodded. "Poached is absolutely fine," I said.

"Eigen is okay," Sill said. "She's enjoying herself. She's never lived before. All she's ever done is stand in front of a whiteboard drawing variables and equations and shit. She might come in handy. You never know."

"How so?" I asked.

"I like to have smart people around me. That's why I like you, Wala. It's not because of your boyish good looks."

"I'm flattered."

"Of course you are. So, who do you think is following you?"

"An apparently very secret government agency. Believe it or not, my shadow is named Bill Clinton."

"You didn't offer to—" He stopped. "Sorry. Bad joke. Let me ask you this: Is he a thirtyish White guy with an eighties haircut?"

"I wouldn't know what that is," I said.

"Short in the front and longer in the back. And he's got a Black partner."

"That's right. How did you know?"

"They're sitting across the street in that baby-blue sedan. Seems rather small for two such big guys."

I looked, saw them, and returned my eyes quickly to the table. "That's them. Do you think they can hear us?"

"Maybe." Sill looked around the room. "They could be pointing a directional microphone at us. They probably are. That's what I'd be doing."

I pulled a pen from my pocket and wrote on a napkin: *How do we lose them?* I wasn't sure why I was asking that, but it made sense. It turned out that I really hated being followed.

Sill raised an index finger, telling me that he had it covered. "Relax, my dear friend," he said.

A woman came in and sat at the counter. There was something familiar about her. She looked slowly around the room. She might have nodded her head toward Sill, but I was unsure. Half a minute later four Sikh men came in and sat at a booth on the other side of the restaurant.

"Put the phone on the table."

I did.

"Leave it there. Here's a new phone."

"Okay."

"I have to hit the head," Sill said. "Be right back."

I sat there alone. The waitress brought the food. I fed a bite of eggs to Trigo. I had no appetite. I looked out the window. Clinton and Mitchell looked like they might even be asleep in the car.

It was not Sill who came back and sat in front of me. It was another slightly brown man and he was wearing Sill's jacket.

"Who are you?" I asked.

"Don't worry about that. It's your turn," he said. When I didn't move, he said, "Go to the washroom." He took a bite of Sill's white toast. "Go on."

"Why?"

"Just go."

I looked at his eyes. He was not threatening, but he was serious. I got up and walked past the old-fashioned cash register and down a short, dirty hallway to the toilet. A Sikh man was waiting in there. Actually it was, at least, a man dressed like a Sikh. He pushed the door closed and faced me.

"Take off your coat and shirt," he said. "I'll hold your dog."

I took off my carrier and handed it and Trigo to him. "What's this all about? What's going on?"

"Sill wants you to do it. Do it."

I slipped out of my jacket and started unbuttoning my shirt.

He put Trigo in a sink and took off his coat and shirt as well. "Do you work for Sill?"

He just smiled.

"Do you?"

"And put on this T-shirt and my jacket."

"Do you?"

"Why do you think I'm exchanging clothes with you in this filthy bathroom?"

"Why do you work for him?" I asked.

"He pays well."

I put on the white T-shirt and the jacket. He took off his turban and placed it on my head. "It's heavy," I said. "What's your name?"

He looked at me quizzically. "Why do you want to know my name?"

"I don't know." That was true. I had no idea why I had asked his name. I suppose I simply wanted to know something.

"My name is Rick James," he said. "Okay? Now go out there and sit at the Sikh table."

I moved to put Trigo back on my chest. "Out there?" I asked.

"No, put the dog in this bag." He pulled out a teddy bear from a gym bag and handed the bag to me.

I put Trigo inside it, apologizing to him as I did. He gave me an accepting look.

The man then put on the carrier and put the teddy bear on his chest.

"To the table," he said. "Go."

I returned to the front of the diner and walked over to the Sikh table as instructed. Sill sat next to me. His turban fit better than mine. In fact, he looked rather handsome with it cocked slightly to the side.

Rick James came from the washroom, went over and sat at our original table, started eating my breakfast. We sat with the men and drank coffee for a few minutes. The waitress noticed the change and was clearly confused, but she said nothing.

"What's going on?" I asked.

"Sikh and ye shall find," Sill said.

The men laughed. They laughed like they were paid to laugh.

I looked at the two men across from me. "My name is Wala," I told them.

They looked at each other, then one said, "Pleased to meet you, Wala. I'm Otis Redding and this here is Barry White."

"Are you also in the villainy business?" I asked.

They looked to Sill and then Otis Redding said, "We're just out enjoying the morning. A stroll by the canal before going to work."

Sill looked at his watch. "Gentlemen."

"Yes."

"Dog's a go," Otis Redding said to Sill.

"Let's do it," Sill said.

Then we all, turbaned men, got up and walked out of the diner and crossed the rather empty street, walked right past the baby-blue sedan. Neither Clinton nor Mitchell gave us even a passing glance. We walked up the hill to M Street. The Sikhs peeled off, walking west, and Sill and I got into a waiting east-pointing limousine. The Mercedes was driven by a woman who never looked back. She said only one thing: "Buckle up, gentlemen. This will be a short ride with no turns."

Sill laughed.

The ride was indeed short and straight.

4

The limo driver delivered us, not surprisingly, safely at the front entrance of the Four Seasons hotel, as if we were any other guests being dropped off, as if we had no reason to concern ourselves with being seen, as if we wanted to be seen. We walked in with parking valets and bell captains flashing smiles and saying, *Good morning, Mr. Sill, How's it going, Mr. Sill,* and *'Sup Sill* from a tattooed young window washer.

"Is this what's known as hiding in plain sight?" I asked.

Sill pulled a couple of black key cards from his shirt breast pocket. "Room 666, your room. Funny, right?"

I faked a laugh, as if I was paid. "I get it."

"Sarcasm," he said. "I didn't know you were capable of sarcasm. But you are, aren't you. It's not a good look. And this other key. Be careful, it looks just like the other one. This is to room 667. Eigen is in there." He looked at his watch. "Or she's in yoga class. Or possibly swimming."

"Okay."

"Anyway. There are clothes in your room for you. Meet you down here in the Bourbon Steak at one for lunch."

"Lunch," I said.

"Everything is moving along beautifully."

I used my key to ride the elevator. There was a woman in the car with me and, as with the woman in the diner, I felt that I had seen her before. She said nothing to me, fairly ignored me. She was still in the car when I exited on the sixth floor. I stood outside Eigen's room and knocked. There was no answer. I thought about the yoga class and the swimming and it didn't sound to me now like she was being held prisoner the way I had been imagining. I had no good reason to enter her room whether she was there or not, so I turned, opened my own door, and walked inside. My room offered a pleasant view of the canal and the river beyond that.

As reported, the closet and drawers were filled with clothes. It amused me to find clothes that were exactly like my wardrobe at home hanging next to suits and a dinner jacket and dress shirts. There were cuff links on the dresser with my initials and a Patek Philippe chronograph. I didn't know much about watches, but from the weight of it I knew that it was expensive.

I lay on the bed with Trigo beside me and stared at the ceiling. I realized my heart was racing and I tried to slow it down. I of course thought of nothing, tried to think of nothing, but that only got me more excited. I turned my mind to the Goldbach conjecture and worked on a proof that I had been building for years. Every time I thought I was close, I would discover a glaring hole in my reasoning, some so obvious as to be embarrassing. It was the problem that fascinated me. I was not at heart a problem solver. This fact was even more evident as I tried to imagine how I might extract myself from this current mess.

Trigo barked just before there was a knock at my door. I got up and looked through the peephole. There was a woman there, dressed in clingy exercise clothes. Her hair was pulled back and her wide-angled face looked familiar. It wasn't until I opened the door that I realized the woman was Gloria. Her afro was gone and she wore makeup. She stepped inside and closed the door, grabbed me by the front of my shirt, and pulled me close. She put her face against mine. After a few seconds I realized this was a kiss.

"What was that for?" I asked.

She didn't answer, but pushed me backward toward the bed. "Gloria, I'm tired. I just drove all the way from Rhode Island." I had a fleeting thought of my car parked on that street off Wisconsin, wondered if it would be towed.

She gave me another headbutt of a kiss and pushed me down on the bed next to Trigo.

"Have you seen Eigen?" I asked.

Trigo didn't growl, bark, or wag his nub at her presence, but rolled over as if to find a napping position. Gloria lay on top of me. Her body was soft and yet it was not. I tried to squirm from under her.

"Don't you want sex?" she asked.

"Not really," I said. "Why would you think I wanted sex?"

She looked at me, her eyes momentarily vacant. "I thought that you were flirting with me on the submarine and I gathered from that that you would want to engage in sexual intercourse with me." She cocked her head slightly. I wondered if that was a sign of embarrassment.

"I wouldn't even know how to flirt with someone," I said.

"You do not find me attractive?" The question was so matter-of-fact. I thought that if I confirmed this statement it wouldn't have mattered to her at all.

"I didn't say that," I said. "Have you seen Eigen?"

"She is in her room."

I looked at Gloria's face. She looked so familiar. "Were you in the diner this morning?"

"No," she said. She stood. "I'll be going now. We have a lot to plan. As I said, Professor Vector is in her room. Lunch will be served at one. Mr. Sill loves lunch." With that she walked to the door and left.

I gave her a minute or two to clear the area, then stepped across the hall to Eigen's room. I knocked. There was no response. I moved to knock again and the door swung open. Eigen was there in a skimpy bright yellow bikini, again looking like a mathematician in a bright yellow bikini.

"Eigen, are you all right?" I asked, following her into the room. Her body was changing, it seemed. I had never looked long and hard at Eigen, but now she seemed slightly longer, perhaps more fit.

"Of course, silly," she said. "I'm perfectly fine. There is a wonderful indoor pool in the hotel. You should try it. Swimming is wonderful exercise."

"I'm sure it is."

"John told me you'd gone back to Providence."

"I was there, but I drove down here last night. I came here because I was worried about you."

"Whatever is there to worry about?"

"Don't you want to come back and finish out the semester? What about your students?"

"Fuck them," she said, sounding nothing like my friend.

"Is that really how you feel? I've never heard you talk like that before." I looked at the nightstand and the surface of the dresser for pill bottles or syringes. "Eigen, has Sill given you any medicines or vitamins and candies?"

"No," she said. "Why would he give me candy? That would be funny, don't you think? I'm not a child, Wala."

"I know you're not."

"John is so alive," she said, all starry-eyed. "Don't you think he's wonderful?" She looked suddenly sleepy. She swayed where she stood, as if in a breeze. I thought she might fall over.

"Are you okay?"

"Just a little tired. I was swimming. Do you like swimming, Wala? The pool here is very nice. It's like a tub, it's so warm. Swimming is a lovely exercise. It's full of geometry. Did you know that?"

"I understand. Maybe you should lie down." I helped her to bed. She was not right. I could see that she was not right.

I really wanted my car now. I knew there was something wrong with Eigen and that if I could only get her away from Sill she would become herself again. And then I thought that maybe I was all wrong.

Anyone else seeing her might have thought that she was simply relaxed and happy. It was all so confusing.

"Have you talked with Gloria at all?" I asked.

"Who is Gloria?"

"We had lunch with her in Corsica. She's tall. She did have big hair, but not now. Now it's pulled back."

"Where is fat face?" she asked.

I was happy to have a glimpse of my friend, but it was terribly brief as she was now asleep. Her head fell back and her mouth opened. She snored. It was the way a person sleeps, nothing extraordinary, but for some reason I found it endearing and it was then that I suspected, though I had little against which to measure it, that I had feelings for Eigen.

5

I left my friend to sleep and returned to my room. I showered and put on clean clothes. I bathed Trigo as well. He always loved that kind of attention. He especially enjoyed lying on his back and soaking. I was letting him do that while I sat beside the tub. I felt the weight of the drive and the morning settle on me and my eyes felt weak, heavy.

"You know," Trigo said, his doggie chin resting on the side of the tub. "Hegel had it turned around. One doesn't start with a thesis. One starts with the antithesis. Everyone always underestimates negation."

"Why are you talking about Hegel?" I asked.

"Kant you see?" he said.

"It's too early in the dream for this, Trigo." I ate from a bowl of ridged potato chips, offered one to my friend. He declined. "What do you think of Sill?" I asked.

"Who?"

"John Sill. The reason we're here."

"Here, now that's a concept."

"Stop, Trigo. I think something is wrong with Eigen."

"Which one is she?"

"The one who calls you fat face."

"Oh, I like her. I don't like being called fat face, but I like her. And she's fucked. Gone. Not right. What happened to her?"

"I don't know," I said.

"You know what I want to know?" Trigo asked.

"What's that?"

"Why do people hate melodrama?"

"What?"

"Is it because they see it as primitive, as not using our sophisticated processes of aesthetic sublimation to manage our fears, needs, and desires, because it works by implementing Manichaeistic strategy? Must our default always be a surrender to our belief in individual psychological complexity?"

"Why do I bother talking to you?"

"It's your dream, human."

"Do you think I need to get her out of here?"

"Are you asking if you should carry out a daring, intrepid, heroic escape? A risk-filled, dangerous, perilous chase where there are unknowns at every turn and straightaway? A shameless, nerve-rattling, out-of-control slide down some treacherous, trigger-taxed, time-sensitive tunnel?"

"Who *are* you?"

"Trigo."

"My question was rhetorical."

"As was my answer," he said. "With overtones of sarcasm. Undertones?"

"Are you saying that attempting an escape with Eigen shows too much or too little imagination?"

"Scratch my belly. And give us one of those chips."

I did both.

"What does *have feelings for* mean?"

"I don't know, Trigo."

"Well, it's not something you need to figure out. A little higher.

Right there. She's our friend, that's all that matters. So, yes to the somewhat predictable car chase. You'll need cash. Go to the ATM and take out a few grand."

"Really?"

"Trust me."

The phone rang. I fell awake on the bed. Trigo lay beneath a fluffy towel beside me, his head on a pillow.

"It's twelve fifty, Mr. Kitu. Your lunch date is at one o'clock." I didn't recognize the male voice.

I sat up, stretched, decided to leave Trigo to sleep peacefully. I found my socks and shoes and stepped across the hall and knocked on Eigen's door. Again and still no answer. I used my key and opened the door. She was not there. I made way downstairs to the Bourbon Steak.

At the table with Sill, Eigen, and Gloria was General Auric Takitall. Sill was dressed for a boating excursion on a warm day. Gloria and Eigen wore red and green skintight leather bodysuits. The general was decked out in full regalia but seemed as comfortable as if he were also dressed for boating.

"Just a couple of minutes late," Sill said, smiling and indicating with a gesture the empty seat across from him. "You remember General Takitall."

"Yes, of course. General. Eigen. Gloria."

Gloria stared right through me, though she didn't appear unhappy.

"We're having pizza," Sill said. "Be here soon. In the meantime why don't you tell the general how you plan to handle our prize once we acquire it."

"You want me to tell him what we're going to do with nothing?"

"Yes."

"Nothing."

Sill smiled at Takitall. "Beautiful, right?"

"The perfect thing about this weapon is that you don't have to arm it, aim it, or fire it. We just sit back and do—" He nodded to me.

"Nothing," I said.

"Nothing," Sill repeated. "Gloria, what do we do?"

"Nothing," she said.

"Nothing." Sill leaned back in his seat and looked at the ornate ceiling. "Hallelujah. It's better than ice cream. And I love ice cream. By the way, they have really great ice cream here. We'll have some after the pizza." He looked at me and then at Takitall. "Of course, before we can sit around letting nothing happen, there is a lot to do."

"That's very true," Takitall said.

"Gloria, just how closely are we being watched? On a scale from one to ten. One being the assholes don't know where the fuck we are, ten being they can smell my farts and count the hairs on my balls."

"Seven," Gloria said. "They know where we are. They know who we're with. They have no idea what we're doing. They are nervous and have been given the green light to shoot us if they want."

Sill feigned fear. "Oh, my. Is it Clinton and Mitchell who are on our proverbial and, dare I say, notorious tails?"

"Yes."

"This should be fun."

"Fun?" I asked.

"They're stupid," he said. "They'll no doubt resort to gunplay because they don't know what we're doing and, well, that's always fun."

"Most of our men are in place," Takitall said.

"Very good," Sill said.

"I want nothing to do with nothing," I said.

"Really?"

"Yes."

"You can have your money back," I said.

"Don't want it. But I still want and expect nothing from you."

"Is he going to be a problem?" the general asked.

Sill shook his head. "But he won't be having pizza. Gloria?"

Gloria showed me the muzzle of a small pistol under the table.

"Professor Wala, you'll go with Gloria now. You've sort of

changed your status in the firm. Not much skin off my ass, but less comfortable for you." Then to Gloria, "Take him upstairs to his room. Let him sit in there and reconsider his position in all of this. Watch a movie or something."

Gloria waved the pistol and I understood her to be telling me to move and so I did. I got up and walked with her out of the restaurant to the elevators, the weapon now out of sight. "What's the plan?" I asked.

She said nothing. The elevator opened and she motioned for me to get in.

"I guess our relationship has changed," I said.

"You might say that," she said, surprising me.

Instead of the sixth floor we went up to the eighth. "My dog is on six," I said.

She did not respond. On the eighth floor she opened a door and stepped aside.

"What's to stop me from leaving?" I asked.

"I'll be standing right here." She positioned herself beside the door.

"My dog is on six," I repeated as the door shut. I leaned against the door, looked through the peephole at her, worried about Trigo. I pounded on the door and said, "I'm ready to have sex now."

6

The room was just like my room, except higher and, of course, guarded. I made a decision as I stood out on the balcony looking at the canal. I would escape. I needed to get to Trigo and I needed to get Eigen away from Sill. Another check at the peephole verified that Gloria was still standing watch. I looked over the rail on the balcony and saw that, predictably, there was a balcony below me. I had to make a decision, that much was clear, especially as I reasoned that doing nothing was in fact a decision, an active decision, not just one by default. If I tried to force my way past Gloria, she would beat me up, perhaps to death, or shoot me, very likely, to death. My remaining option was the window. The balcony below me was my target of course. I climbed over the rail and lowered my body. I did so rather quickly, either because of a disregard or lack of comprehension about the danger of my undertaking or because of an undeniable lack of physical prowess. Whatever, I found myself hanging by my fingernails some eight floors above a sidewalk and fence. One thing was certain. There was no turning back. The suspense here is strange, as of course one would know that I did not fall to my death, though I suppose it is possible that I could have survived to write this from my wheelchair or that life as we understand it is wrong, like in a cartoon world where characters bounce and then reassemble. But forget that. I swung there. I might have peed a little. I peed a little. I put some effort into my swinging and let go. I landed on the balcony of a woman and a man who were engaged in sex in the bed. I stepped into the room and put a finger to my pursed lips.

"Please, don't scream," I said.

Well, that didn't work.

She did scream. The man stood up naked from the bed, pulling the sheet from the woman. She tugged back. He didn't want to have anything to do with me.

I moved quickly to the door. "I'm going. Please be quiet. I have no interest in either of you."

The woman stopped screaming as I reached for the door. "Where'd he come from? Where did he come from?" she asked.

"The window," the man said.

The woman and I paused at his response. I muttered another apology and stepped into the empty corridor. If I was any kind of mathematician, then I was correct to assume that I was now on the seventh floor. I found the stairs and went down to my floor and room. I put Trigo into the gym bag and crossed the hall to Eigen's room. We waited in her closet.

An hour went by and I must have dozed because I was startled alert by Gloria's voice saying, "He's not here. He's left the hotel."

I peeked out to see that she was making her report over the phone.

"Yes, he has his dog," she said.

Eigen was seated on the bed behind her. She unzipped the front of her bodysuit and fell back, stared at the ceiling.

"I'll go out and walk along the canal, see if I can find him." Gloria ended the call and walked out of the room.

I waited a few minutes, in which time I believed that Eigen had drifted to sleep. I stood over her, said her name softly. Again. I put Trigo on the bed next to her and took a look into the hallway. Then I went to her window and looked down at M Street.

"Oh, fat face," I heard her say. I turned to find her holding him.

"Eigen, we're getting out of here."

"I think that's a good idea," she said. "Wala, I don't feel so good."

"Do you have any clothes that are more understated? You're rather easy to spot dressed like that.

"Yes."

"Good. Get changed and I'll be right back." While she changed, I went back into my room and pulled a light gray suit from the closet. I put on a dress shirt with no tie and slipped into dress shoes. I forgot socks, but I didn't care. Back in Eigen's room I was surprised to find her ready to go. She was wearing a simple yellow dress and sandals. She looked like her usual kind and gentle self and was suddenly pretty. A condition that might have always existed, but I was just now seeing it.

"We have to go," I said.

"You look funny," she said.

"I know," I said. "I feel funny. Okay, we're just going to walk calmly out of the hotel and into Georgetown and try to find my car. Just keep your head down."

She dropped her chin to her chest.

"Not that far down. You're not to look like I beat you." I realized at that moment that my manner of addressing Eigen had changed. I was at once more direct and less parental. "Let's go."

"Wala, I'm afraid."

"Yes, I know. So am I."

A distinction between names and other words

1

Eigen and I managed to get out of the hotel without seeing Gloria and I assumed without being seen by her. I was reminded that what we see is really all we know; everything else is induction, deduction, or simple guesswork. You drive by cattle in a pasture and you think brown cows and then you think further that at the very least they are brown on one side. But just a few strides west put us in view of several Sikh-appearing men. I turned us around and we walked toward a bridge. There was a steady stream of pedestrians and cars and so, dressed as we were, I thought we were fairly well camouflaged. The air was cool and I realized that in our haste we had forgotten a wrap for Eigen. I took off my suit coat and put it around her, a gesture that felt both necessary and correct and strangely intimate. At an ATM just blocks from the hotel I removed a sizable amount of cash from my account. Being close to the hotel didn't give away much. Soon we were at the Foggy Bottom Metro station. We got on a blue line train and sat. We hadn't spoken since we left the hotel.

"Are you okay?" I asked.

"I'm so stupid," Eigen said.

"I don't think anyone would say that," I said. "How many people actually understand the Collatz conjecture?"

"That doesn't mean anything. That's just a game. I don't know anything about"—she paused—"life."

"Neither of us."

"You came back for me," she said.

"You're my friend."

"I don't remember much of anything."

"I think you were drugged."

"Where are we going?"

"I'm going to try to get you back to Providence."

"What about you?"

"I don't know." I remembered that I was still carrying the new phone that Sill had given me in the diner. I slipped it into the open tote bag off a woman who was exiting the train at the Smithsonian stop. "I don't know," I said, again. "Sill wants me for nothing, though I don't know what that comes to. The government wants me because they're afraid of Sill. I believe they are all dangerous."

Trigo poked his head out of the bag. I gently stuffed him back inside. "I know, boy. You're hungry."

"This is crazy," Eigen said, looking around.

"It's no use looking around. If they see us, they see us. We'll never recognize any of them. The government might want to shoot me on sight. At least that's the way Sill made it sound."

"What does he want?"

"He wants to make America nothing again." I looked up at the Metro system map. "We'll get off here at L'Enfant Plaza and take the yellow line up to the red line to Union Station."

"You're very capable," Eigen said.

"Don't fool yourself. We're just alike. We can calculate the cube roots of seven-digit numbers in our heads, but we can't balance a checkbook. I'm even worse, I can understand that paradoxes are necessary for language to actually work in the world, but I can't see a lie that is staring me in the face."

"Why does he want you?" she asked.

"I wish I could tell you. I viewed it all as a joke at first. I still do,

I suppose. Supposedly I am an expert in nothing and that's why he wants me."

"But you are an expert in nothing."

"I can't argue with you. It's true that if there's one thing I know, it's nothing."

The train stopped and we got out. On our way to the next train I thought I saw Gloria. It was a brief glimpse and then the face was gone, but it was more than enough to spook me and so I led us out of the Metro and onto the street. We were now in Chinatown.

"You're planning on sending me back to Providence alone," she said.

We were standing in front of a Chinese restaurant called Meiyou. I looked at the dead, plucked, and uncooked ducks sitting in the window.

"Wala?"

"I want you to be safe."

"I need to find out what Sill is really doing. I need to know."

"I want to stay with you and Trigo."

I looked at the restaurant menu displayed outside, remembered that I never had pizza. "Let's grab a bite. Trigo is hungry and so am I. Aren't you hungry? Of course you are. We'll sit and rest and figure this out."

We sat at a table away from the window, but where I could see out. I pulled Trigo into my lap as we looked at the menus.

The waiter saw Trigo and came quickly over. "I'm sorry, but we do not allow pets in the restaurant. He can wait outside. People usually tie their dogs to the bike rack."

"I can't do that," I said. I held Trigo up for inspection.

"Your dog has no legs," he said.

"He has one," I said.

The waiter looked around the restaurant and then back toward the kitchen. "I've never seen anything like that. You must love your dog very much."

"I do."

"He does," Eigen said.

"What is his name?"

"Trigo."

"What does it mean?"

"In Spanish it means wheat," I said. "It can also refer to the number three. But actually it doesn't mean anything. It's his name."

"Names always mean something," the waiter said. "My name is Yingjie. It means brave hero."

"My name is Wala. It means nothing."

"And your name?" the waiter spoke to Eigen. "What does your name mean?"

"My name is Eigen. Private."

"I will be back for your orders," he said.

"He didn't seem happy," Eigen said.

"I think he didn't like our names."

"What was I doing, Wala?"

"You said you wanted to be bad," I told her. "And I kind of got it."

"I remember that much. I'm such a fool."

"We're both fools. Maybe we're all fools."

2

Eigen Vector's mother was a famous botanist, as fame goes in the world of botany. Names like Carolus Linnaeus and Charles Bessey don't roll off the tongue. Perhaps Mendel and his peas. Perhaps the name George Washington Carver might have rung a bell, a great botanist relegated to second-order recognition, being called an agricultural scientist. Daisy Vector, née Meyerowitz, was an expert on Asteraceae. She was the author of *Flora of the Southwest* and four plant genera of the aster family were named for her. She was at best an absent mother, not without love for her daughter, but also not the least bit unwilling to leave her in the care of a young Hungarian nanny named Zsóphia Szabó. Richard Vector was a well-known sculptor, known best and perhaps solely for a giant public work of art that was taken down due to outrage. The metal work depicted a not much abstracted form of an enormous penis in mid-circumcision. The city of Omaha, Nebraska, was, to a person, unhappy with the dick that Dick built. It turned out that nothing could have been better for his career, as he became instantly famous and never worked again. He was at home with his daughter as little as his wife and it turned out that enormous metal penises were not the only kind he was willing to share. He shared his more modest fleshy one with Zsóphia Szabó on more than a few occasions.

Daisy and Dick staged a rather loud and public divorce, neither offering much comfort to their quiet, genius, tucked-away child. She was thirteen and it all crashed down on her and so she attempted suicide. Eigen Vector leaped from a highway bridge over a river in Ithaca, New York, leading to the memorable headline: Depressed Daughter of Dick and Daisy Dives into Drink. Her parents were scared or shamed into remaining together for the sake of the child, creating a sour home with intense and crippling attention focused on the daughter. Eigen spiraled inward, finding mathematics along the way, a world that her parents could not penetrate and so became hers and hers alone. The daughter of Daisy and Dick was in graduate school at Caltech at the age of sixteen and a tenured professor at Brown at nineteen.

"You can't send me back alone," Eigen said, holding an egg roll expertly between chopsticks.

"Your reasoning?"

"Because you need my help."

"And why do you say that?"

"If you're so unsure of the situation that you need to send me away, then you obviously need my help figuring out this situation. If your main concern is my safety, then you need to know that I am safe and the only way to know that is if I am with you." She smiled.

"I see you're dining with Morton's fork. Okay, but we still need to go to the train station. I want Sill to at least think that you or both of us are headed back to Providence."

"What's our plan?"

Eigen's voice, her demeanor had changed. She was less timid, more focused. She even consumed her food with more vigor.

She caught the waiter as he passed. "This soup is fantastic. What is it called?"

He looked at both of us and said, "It has no name."

"It must have a name," she said.

"Really?" The waiter walked away.

"He doesn't like us," Eigen said.

"But he's right," I said.

"What do you mean?"

"Why does it have to have a name?" I asked. "There is no logical necessity for a thing to be named."

"Then how can we refer to it?"

"Everything that is a thing is named. Everything that is not a thing is not named."

Eigen stared into space. "I don't understand."

"And you shouldn't," I said.

"I know what I need to do or rather where I need to be. I need to be there so that I can see nothing."

"I'm lost."

The waiter came with the check.

"I want to thank you," I said.

"For what?"

"For nothing."

I could see him becoming angry.

"You don't understand," I said. "You've pointed out what I should have seen all along. Everything is about naming."

"Here's your check. The soup was on the house."

3

I hailed a taxi. Actually, Eigen hailed the taxi, as none would stop when I tried. And we made our way to the train station. There I made a point of walking past as many cameras as possible; I used the ATM again and stood chatting with the clerk as I bought two one-way tickets to Providence. We bought hooded sweatshirts and some sweatpants for Eigen that, strangely, had the word *juicy* written across the backside. She put them on in the washroom and then we stood in line to board. As the crowd congealed, we pulled up our hoods and walked away in a tangled herd of arriving passengers. Outside, the daylight was waning and the air was considerably colder. We walked straight away south and into Columbus Circle. A street preacher in tattered clothes stood on an actual soapbox and held forth. The wooden crate on which he stood read *Tide.*

"You there," he said, pointing at me. "You there. Do you have a recollection of the direction that your introspection has allowed recognition? If you have suffered insinuation into a situation that is not of your propagation, then you must take my invitation to meet our savior the Lord Jesus Christ, hallelujah amen can I get a witness?" When no one responded he said, "Can I get a goddamn witness, motherfucker?!"

A homeless man lying on a nearby park bench raised his arm and said, "Preach, brother."

"Amen. Where is life taking you, sister?" The preacher looked at Eigen.

"I don't know," she said.

"She doesn't know. How many times have I heard that. The repetition of the elocution of that rendition of proclamation leaves me wanting explanation. It is my contention that the asseveration of your location vis-à-vis your position remains without explanation in spite of my verbalization, my vocalization, my ejaculation of the problemation. Amen hallelujah can I get a witness?"

"Preach, brother."

"Is that a dog in that bag?" the preacher asked.

"Yes," I said.

"Jesus had a dog. Very few people know that."

"What kind of dog did Jesus have?" I asked.

"A Chihuahua. Named Jeremiah."

"My dog is named Trigo."

"Can I tell you one thing, brother?"

I nodded.

"Just remember this. If you forget everything else, remember this. If you awake and don't know nothing about nothing, know this. Are you ready? Are you ready, son? Are you ready to hear it?"

"I am," I said.

"Will you remember it?"

"I will."

"Hallelujah." He looked around and then leaned slightly forward. I thought he might fall off his Tide box. He said, "Negation is affirmation, but neutralization, nullification, and, dare I say, even repudiation are not the same as nonexistence."

The witness on the bench sat up. "You mean nonexistiation."

"So right, brother. A benediction for your rectification." He pointed to Eigen and me. "Remember that the actuality and veracity and factuality of this recognition and legislation is that I am

nobody. You am nobody. All God's children am nobody. Say it with
me, I am nobody! Now sing it with me!

> "I am nobody and nobody is me
> Walking the land or swimming the sea
> Searching for Jesus or Allah or Buddha
> Shiva for you and Vishnu for me

> "I am nobody as nobody can see
> Tremblings from the heavens on high
> No answers will find us, we are done
> We is borned, we is loved, we cry, we die

"Amen hallelujah can I get a motherfuckin' witness?!"

We left the preacher and walked west along Massachusetts
Avenue.

"Wala, what are we doing? We're just a couple of math professors. Shouldn't we go to the police?"

"And tell them what?"

"I don't know."

"I've met the authorities. They're worse than Sill. I'm not even
certain that I saw him kill that man."

"Kill?" Eigen stopped in her tracks.

"In Miami. We were sitting at the table and the floor opened up
and down he went. A Brazilian man."

"I don't remember that at all."

"Gloria told me he was fed to sharks," I said.

"Who is Gloria?"

Not being able to recall these things was causing Eigen to feel
considerable anxiety. "We need a place to sleep," I said. A Holiday Inn
sign was brightly lit a block away. "We can get a room there."

4

We secured a room with cash. It turned out the motel was a hub of illegal activity. I was in no way street savvy and, in fact, when it came to reading the workings of the world in general, I was just this side of illiterate, but even I could see drug deals that were not covert and even I could spot hookers who wore orange fishnets and price tags pinned to their breasts. As poorly read as I was, Eigen didn't even know the alphabet. She greeted each and every person on the way to our smoke-sour petri dish of a room with a bright *How are you?* As dirty as our room was, the crusted carpet, the stained bedcover, the aforementioned smoke, the washroom was surprisingly clean. That was something. I pulled the cover off the bed and let Trigo out of the bag.

"You should take a shower," I said. "Try to relax."

"Why can't I remember things?" she asked.

"I don't know, Eigen. Do you remember being given any pills or anything strange to drink?"

"No. At least I remember you." She smiled.

"A shower will help you feel better. At least the bathroom looks clean."

"Are we in danger, Wala?"

"I honestly don't know. I think so."

Eigen yawned.

"You must be exhausted."

"I am," she said. "You, too?"

I nodded. "I'll get cleaned up after you."

I lay back next to Trigo while Eigen was in the shower.

It is not easy to judge the value of a problem with any confidence in advance. We can ask if there are necessary and sufficient conditions satisfied for identifying something as a problem. I had always considered, in regard to math, that in order for something to be a problem, when stated it should make complete and total sense to the first person one meets on the street. The problem should be perfect and clean. Such was not the case at that moment. Not only could I not articulate the problem or represent it symbolically, but I could not even be certain that the problem was real and significant.

After a while Eigen came out of the washroom laughing. "Look at this," she said. She was holding a small plastic bottle of shampoo.

"What about it?"

"Look at the name."

I took it from her and looked at the label. *Young-Laplace.* "That's great," I said. The Young-Laplace equation was a nonlinear partial differential equation that described capillary pressure that had application regarding the surface of soap bubbles. I looked at Eigen, my friend, with new appreciation. What was wonderful was how unfunny this association was, how many connections she had to traverse to find the humor. Her eyes looked so tired. "You take the bed. I'll sleep on the floor."

"No," she said.

"It's fine. I sometimes do it at home. It makes my back feel better."

"I think I'm scared to sleep alone in the bed."

"I'll be right here. First, a shower for me. You can keep Trigo company. He'll be in bed with you."

"Fat face."

The shower felt good. I can't say that it actually cleared my head, but at least it afforded me some minutes when I didn't think. Back in the room Eigen was asleep and so was Trigo. I found an extra blanket in the closet, took a pillow from the bed. I wrapped myself in the blanket, not wanting to put my skin against the carpet. My attempt at sleep was protracted by the constant squeaking of nearby beds and the half-hearted, unenthusiastic moaning of dead-eyed prostitutes. *Yeah, baby. Give it to me, baby. It's so big, baby. Come, already, baby. No, no, nonono, wrong hole, baby. How much?*

Trigo leaned his fat face over the edge of the bed. "You do realize that this is all about surfaces. You know that, right? That's what Eigen was unconsciously trying to tell you with the shampoo talk. She's far smarter than both of us, but she doesn't know it. It's endearing, isn't it?"

"I guess. If you say so," I said. "Sometimes it's exhausting."

"Tell me, please, what good thing isn't exhausting? Surfaces are where it's at, as the kids say."

"What kids?"

"You know, the proverbial ones, the television ones, that's what they say. It's cool, dope, stupid. You know. Anyway, think surfaces. Rational surfaces, Hirzebruch surfaces, hyperelliptic surfaces, nodal Picard modular, Campedelli, and algebraic surfaces. Remember, a surface by definition has no depth, only planar existence."

"You're making that up."

"You bet your sweet non-Euclidean ass I'm making it up. I'm a dog. I can't read. Unlike the world at large, my imagination is surface all the way to the very bottom. You can try to place a ruled surface on my projective line all you want, but that will get you nowhere. Heraclitus, there a clitus, everywhere a clitus."

"I don't get it," I said.

"Unlike rivers, one can in fact step in the same shit twice." Trigo barked out a laugh. "We have about one day, three hours, and sixteen minutes before you need to know how to handle this situation. You have to stop Sill from accessing that complex projective plane orbiter. Impressed that I remember that?"

"Not particularly, but you're right, of course. I have to be ready for everything, but especially ready for nothing. If I can be there and affirm nothing and so negate it, then Sill will have nothing, rather he will not have nothing, or, at least, less than he started with or more than he wants."

"And Bingo was his name-o," the dog sang. "Imagine that entity than which none less can be conceived. It is better to be nothing than to not exist. Therefore, accordingly, ergo, even hence, nothing is God and God is nothing."

"You left out *thus* and *consequently.*"

"My bad."

"Trigo, why I am I bothering to try to stop him?"

"It's a pickle," he said.

"What? What do you mean?"

"I mean it's a pickle." Trigo held a gherkin between the toes of his one paw. "It's a pickle," he said and ate it.

"Where did you get a pickle?"

"This is a dream, Wala."

"Oh, yeah."

"Pickles are more square because pickles have no hair. You can eat them in the closet, you can eat them anywhere."

We let that hang dreamily in the air for a bit.

"What if Sill is actually able to direct nothing at New York," I said. "What if he negates the nation's largest city?"

"More room for you and more room for me, a chicken in every pot, pigeons in the sea. Sorry, there's nothing funny about that."

"What are the odds?" I asked. "That's a long way for nothing to travel. I mean, what if nothing gets in its way? And what if nothing doesn't arrive?"

"Well, then nothing will happen."

"That's exactly what I'm afraid of."

"Then it appears to me that you are prepared. You have absolutely nothing to worry about."

5

Morning came, as mornings come. If there was a lull in the squeaking and moaning and bartering, I slept right through it. Eigen and Trigo were still sleeping peacefully as I walked over to the window and looked down at the parking lot. Men walked swiftly, heads down, to their cars. A police cruiser drove through without stopping. I entertained for a second that they were looking for us. The feeling underscored my paranoia, as if my paranoia needed underscoring. Anyway, my feeling was not paranoia, as I was clearly not exhibiting any sort of attribution bias. There were in fact people following me and looking for me and desiring my company for nefarious or other reasons. Paranoia would have me think that Eigen had been allowed to escape with me so that they would know where I was. But of course that was certainly, patently, assuredly untrue. I turned to see her sleeping there with Trigo's heavy head resting on her belly.

I sat on the only chair in the room, a desk chair on wheels, and contemplated my next move. I then remembered a strange, eccentric acquaintance I had made some years back, an alcoholic Catholic priest who was in fact an atheist. He had at one time taught at Georgetown, but had since moved to Catholic University, a lesser school, but the administration fairly ignored him. I couldn't remember the man's name, only that he, being an atheistic nihilist, showed some interest in my study of nothing. He was at once reserved and without boundaries. I suspected that, like me, he was somewhere on the spectrum. Enough to make him awkward and unwanted, but not enough to have his behavior be excused. He in fact had had some ideas on the subject, ideas that amounted to, well, you guessed it.

"Wala?" Eigen opened her eyes and found me. She reached down and found Trigo's fat face. "How long have you been up?"

"Just awhile."

"I must have been really exhausted," she said. Panting, grunting, and wall slapping came from the adjacent room. "Did that go on all night?"

"I believe so," I said. "If not from that room, then from others. Things seem to have slowed down a bit. Getting close to checkout time."

"Are they hookers?" She whispered the last word.

I nodded.

She laughed. "Cool."

I nodded.

"What do we do today?" she asked. She sat up. "Let me give the boy a nice caress." She stroked Trigo's belly and one of his nubs shook.

"That's it," I said.

"What's it?"

"The name. Karras, that's his name. Damien Karras."

"Who's that?"

"He might be able to help us. He's a priest. But he's also an astrophysicist."

"I don't like priests," she said.

I was surprised by her remark. I had never heard her say she disliked anything or anyone. "Why do you dislike priests?"

"Because of what they do to children."

"Not all priest are pedophiles," I said.

"No, but they all teach them lies. When I was a child and my parents weren't around, a priest told me to pray and everything would be all right. It wasn't all right. When I was depressed and needed help, another priest told me that God would take care of me. God didn't. Priests lie to children."

"You might be relieved to know that this priest doesn't believe in God or Jesus or the Mother Mary."

"What does he believe in?"

"He believes in gin. He believes in rum. He believes in bourbon. He might believe in beer and wine."

Eigen stared at me.

"He believes in nothing."

The Holiday Inn was relatively quiet now. The whole structure seemed to snore. We walked past the sleeping desk clerk and out onto Massachusetts Avenue, where we grabbed a taxi. The campus of Catholic University was larger than I thought it might be. We asked brother after robed brother and student after student and not one of them knew of a Father Karras. Then I remembered something I'd learned years earlier: if you want to know about a place, ask a custodian. And so I did.

"Yeah, I know Father Karras," he said. "His office ain't around here."

"Where is it?" I asked.

He looked at his oversized pocket watch, then appeared to verify its reading by looking at the sun. "Well, okay, I'll take you there, but we'll have to walk fast."

"We'll keep up."

"Father Karras doesn't get many people looking for him," the man said. "In fact, I can't remember anyone coming to look for him. His rooms are next to his office, so he doesn't come out much."

He led us to the far edge of the campus, past an old gymnasium and to a raggedy, two-level building next to the physical plant.

"He's inside there, top of the stairs," the man said over the stuttering roar of machinery. He checked his watch again.

I thanked him and watched him trot away.

The large dirty windows let in dirty light that filled a large dirty room. A single heavy punching bag hung from a thick pipe on the ceiling. We walked up the metal stairs to the second level, a mezzanine that wrapped around the perimeter of the building. A sign on the first door read Karras. I knocked.

The door swung open. A sixty-year-old man faced us, thick gray brows hovered over his bloodshot eyes, his face set in a frown. He was dressed in a frock and collar and no trousers. "What do you want?"

"Father Karras? Damien Karras?"

He focused. "I know you," he said. "You're the nothing guy."

"Wala Kitu."

"Yeah, I remember. That was back when my research meant a goddamn to me. Chicago, right?"

I nodded.

"What the fucking hell are you doing here?" He looked at Eigen. "And just who might you be, you beautiful creature?" he said. "Is that sexist of me to call a young lady a creature, because if it is, I'm fucking sorry. Shit."

"I don't know," I said. "Probably. Yes, it is. This is Eigen Vector. Listen, we need your help."

Those words stopped him. "My help? No fucking one has needed my help since—well, not for a long goddamn time. What could I possibly do for you?"

"To tell the truth, I don't know."

"I should put on some fucking pants." He fell back into his quarters and grabbed black pants from a chair, stepping into them while he looked at us. "You need somebody exorcised or some shit?"

"I wouldn't mind seeing that, but no," I said.

"Is that a dog in the bag?"

"Trigo," I said.

"Why the fuck is he in the bag?"

"He has only one leg."

"You see, that's goddamn God for you," he said.

"Is it true you don't believe in God?" Eigen asked.

"Yes, fucking true," he said.

"What do you believe in?"

"I believe in the goddamn devil."

"You worship the devil?"

"Hell no. But I believe he exists. Maybe God does, too. But if he does, then he's a goddamn alcoholic like me. Well, not exactly like me. He doesn't give a shit. Or he's a fucking idiot."

"Do you give a shit?" Eigen asked.

"In my way." Karras smiled. "In my way."

"I saw the bag downstairs," I said. "Do you still box?"

"I hit the bag. Why, you need some muscle?" He threw out a couple of punches, bobbed and weaved.

"We might," I said. "Do you remember my work on nothing?"

"Sort of. I can't say I fucking understood it even then."

"Someone is seeking to harness that power." The words sounded stupid in my mouth and worse in the air. "I don't really know why I'm here, Father Karras."

"Damien."

I nodded. "I need to get into the Naval Observatory tonight. I know you used to use the equipment there."

"Before I ask why, I'll say it can't be done. Motherfucking vice president lives there or on campus thereabouts."

"I was in the telescope room two nights ago."

"Really? On a tour?"

"No, in the middle of the night, just three of us. I was there with a man named John Sill and an astronomer name Jean Luc."

"Monfils," he said with me. "Giant Haitian."

I nodded.

"Smart, but he might be evil. Of course I think everyone might be evil." He walked to his little kitchen table and filled a glass with bourbon, drank it straight down as if it were juice. "Lunch."

"You're an astronomer?" Eigen asked.

Karras looked at the glass in his hand. "I am. Specifically, a cosmologist. I've spent my entire pitiful life thinking about cosmic inflation. And one wonders why I drink. When I started my studies, I thought I would find God in the stars."

"You didn't?" she asked.

"It's just a bunch of burning gases out there. It's all very pretty, I'll give you that. Sit down." He pointed to chairs at his small table. "I won't offer you this stuff, but would you like tea?"

"I'd like tea," Eigen said.

"Please," I said.

Karras filled a saucepan with water and put it on the electric stove top. "I hate electric, but they won't trust me with gas. Think I'll blow up the school."

"Why are you a priest?" Eigen asked.

"I used to believe in God, but then I saw evil. You simply can't fucking have both in the same world. That's why I was interested in your damn work back then." He smiled at me. "Not that I am comparing evil to nothing."

"Of course," I said. "The government has hidden some kind of craft in space. It carries a telescope as powerful as the Hubble and it's pointed at earth."

"I see," he said.

"It's using a disguised communication satellite as a relay to deliver its intel to Earth. It may also be true that they have found nothing."

"You still contend that what you mean by nothing is not the same as antimatter," he said.

"Nor is it dark matter," I said.

He shook his head, looked at Eigen. "One of the things that stumps us is how there can be so much more matter than antimatter in the observable world."

"Yes, you can ask that question," I said.

"Fucking right," he said.

"But there is more nothing than anything else and it is not observable at all."

Eigen took a mug of tea from Karras. "How do you know there is nothing, Wala?"

"What did you just ask me about?"

"Nothing," he said.

"There it is. Nothing is everywhere and nowhere. It exists all the time and at no time. It doesn't change or move and experience or exhibit any kind of change, so time is unintelligible when considering it. Nothing is so dangerous." I looked out the window. "Tell Eigen how you saw evil."

He stared at me for a few beats and then nodded. "I performed an exorcism in my youth. I had to drive fucking evil out of a little girl. The experience rocked my faith, took it from me, showed me that there can be no God."

"How do you hide something in space?" I asked.

"You put it behind something," Karras said. "But there is nothing to hide behind out there."

"Why are you still a priest?" Eigen asked, not letting the subject go.

"My dear girl," Karras said. "I remain a goddamn cleric because in this world one needs something to hide behind. I have chosen this fucking collar. You have chosen mathematics."

"How did you know I'm a mathematician?"

"You're hanging out with him." Karras pointed at me. "Your name is Eigen Vector. I might be a priest, but I'm not fucking stupid."

Chasing two rabbits

1

From passage to pastiche was how I might have characterized the last two days, though I wasn't sure why. Father Karras assured us that while he might have been dressed, he was not clean and asked us to wait downstairs while he performed his ablutions. When Eigen turned to the door, Karras looked at the seat of her sweatpants. "Juicy."

"What?" Eigen turned around.

"Your pants say *juicy* on the butt," he said.

She tried to look back. "They do? Wala, why didn't you tell me?"

"I didn't think it mattered. And we were in a hurry."

"Whatever does that mean?" she asked.

"I don't know," I said.

"I don't think it's good," she said.

"You can have a pair of my sweatpants," Karras said.

"Those do make you easy to spot," I said.

The sweatpants that Karras gave Eigen pretty much swallowed her. She was just able to cinch them tight enough with the drawstring, but they were voluminous. She was even more conspicuous now.

"How is this?" she asked.

"Good," I lied.

"Nothing's written back there," she said as a question.

"Only *Jesus Saves*," Karras said.

"What?" Eigen said.

"Just joking," he said. "Jesus never saved any-fucking-body."

Eigen and I waited downstairs by the heavy bag. She punched it with a loose fist and felt some pain.

"How does anybody hit that?" she asked.

"Shift your weight to your back leg as you twist hard and pivot onto the ball of your front foot. Simultaneously, swing your left arm forward with your elbow bent at about ninety degrees and turn your hips with your motion. Keep your fist closed and let your palm face the floor."

"How do you know this?" she asked.

"I read it."

She tried as I held the bag. "Still hurts."

"It's going to hurt. That's just the beginning. The faster you turn your hips, the more power you will generate. But the real force comes from the delivery and the release."

"I don't get it."

"When your fist hits the bag, let your body move through it. Then let everything go."

"I don't understand."

"To tell the truth, neither do I. I try not to hit things."

She hit the bag again. She shook her hand in pain.

"That's why," I said.

Father Karras came down in a fresh set of priest pants, frock, and collar. With him dressed so, with Eigen swimming in gray sweatpants cinched at the middle and rolled at the legs and hooded sweatshirt, and with me in my suit, we looked crazy.

"Where to?" I asked.

"The Kenyon Grill," Karras said. "I'm hungry. I'm sure you two are as well."

We walked to his car, a midseventies Chevy Malibu. The vinyl top had long baked off and left a shell of a roof that didn't match the body. After three tries, it started with a cough and a bang.

"It's the unleaded gas," Karras said.

"Why the Kenyon Grill?" I asked.

"I like the food."

The restaurant was near Howard University and it was crowded. Despite our appearance no one paid any attention to us. Until I noticed a woman cutting us glances from a booth by the door. I never saw more than a quarter of her profile, but she looked familiar. Finally, I asked Eigen to take a look at her.

"By the door, in the booth. Have you seen her before?"

"Who?" she asked.

"The woman over there."

"There is no woman over there," she said.

I looked again and the booth was empty.

The waitress, an older woman, came over, poised her pencil over her pad. "What in the h-e-l-l do you want? Is that a dog?"

"Yes," I said. "My dog."

"We don't allow dogs in here."

"He's only got one leg," I said.

"I don't care if he's got two d-i-c-k-s. No dogs."

"Look at his fat face," Eigen said.

The waitress did. Trigo gave up his fattest, big-eyed face.

"Okay, he's cute. He can stay," she said. "Again, what in the h-e-l-l do you want to eat?"

"I'll have the f-u-c-k-i-n-g chili," Karras said.

She looked to Eigen and me.

We agreed to chili, also.

"So, you like the food here," I said.

Karras shrugged. "I like the ambience. Kitu, how many people have you told about this? That you were in the fucking observatory."

"No one. Why?"

"Just wondering. What's your goddamn plan?"

"I don't have one. I came to you because you know your way around there. I imagine that if I can be there when Sill tries to harness nothing, my observational pressure will have negative and therefore positive effect."

Karras nodded. "Then we'll fucking get you in there."

"Why do you swear so much?" Eigen asked Karras.

"Fuck, do I?"

"A lot. It doesn't bother me, but I was wondering."

"Maybe it's because one night long ago I had to fucking watch a goddamn preteen fuck her own pussy bloody with a cruci-fucking-fix while she screamed at me that my fucking sweet, dead mother was sucking cocks in hell." Karras pulled a flask from his frock pocket and took a swig. "Goddamn exorcisms."

His saying all of this to Eigen was bad enough, but he had said it loud enough for everyone in the restaurant to hear. To understate it justly, every set of eyes in the restaurant was settled on him.

"What's everybody fucking looking at? What are you fucking looking at? Haven't you ever seen a goddamn priest before?"

The patrons went back to their meals. The waitress came and stood over Karras, hands on hips.

"What in the h-e-l-l is wrong with you?"

"I did not have the f-u-c-k-i-n-g energy to spell out every g-o-d-d-a-m-n word. Won't happen again," Karras said.

"It better the fuck not," she said.

2

Karras was adamant that the best way into the Naval Observatory was the legal way, a public tour. If we were caught on the grounds, we would likely be arrested by the Secret Service, and since I didn't have an ancient key like Sill, being caught was a near certainty. He parked the Malibu not far from where my car had been parked before it was towed. Finding the BMW was going to be impossible, as I had no license, no registration, no idea of the plate number and could not remember the model, year, or color. Given that, it could have been parked three spaces away and I would not have known.

Gaining entry was easy enough. We bought tickets and walked in. "Easy peasy," Karras said. We walked through a room of clocks, read plaques about time, visited the library, and then looked at the telescope. We stayed with the tour group, which consisted of a couple from Ames, Iowa, and their six children from six to fifteen; a young gay German couple who seemed to be in the middle of breaking up; a man from Albany, New York, who wore a jacket with patches from every national park in the country and every tourist site in the District of Columbia; and a pair of librarians from Falls Church, Virginia, who visited the observatory weekly because they had a crush on the docent, a sixty-three-year-old retired navy commander with sideburns and impeccable posture. As the tour was near complete, Karras peeled us off and we slipped back into the circular library. Eigen and I followed him past the rope that forbade tourists to climb the stairs to the mezzanine. Once up there with the beautiful, old books, he had us lie on the floor so that we were concealed by the half wall.

"What now?" I asked.

"I suggest a nap," Karras said. "No-fucking-body comes up here and they'll be locking up soon. We'll get up, go to the telescope room, find the fucking thingie out there in space and you can do what you have to goddamn do. So, nighty-night."

Trigo pushed his head out of the bag. "Wala."

"What? I'm trying to sleep. I need to sleep. I need to be rested."

"You are asleep," the dog said. "Something's not right. Getting in here was too easy, don't you think?"

"Now that you mention it," I said. "What are you thinking?"

"I'm thinking that in the *Apology* Socrates's irony is actually ironic. And I mean that sincerely."

"What?"

"We've been betrayed."

"We have?"

"Remember that pickle?"

"Yes. Why are we talking about that pickle?"

"That was a good pickle. I really liked that pickle. That pickle gave me terrible gas. I have felt bad all day. I wouldn't stick my face in this bag if I were you."

I stared at him.

"The pickle talk is metaphor. Get it?"

"Was it a metaphor the first time you said it?" I asked.

"Who knows. A madman doesn't speak in his own voice, you know. So it's anyone's guess what your dreaming is all about. There is some, let's call it interstitial, space between madness and nonsense that you and I have yet to map out. But know this, things are headed south."

3

I was lying awake now, imagining our sneaking into the telescope room, where I would peer through the eyepiece and see the stream of nothing coming from deep space and render it *something* with observational pressure. The tricky part was that one had to know that one was observing nothing for the pressure to have effect and realize at the same time that there was nothing to observe in the first place. I heard the movement of furniture below us on the library floor. I sat up to peek over the half wall.

Applause. Clapping from about twenty men in suits, among them John Sill and Gloria. Seated was a plastic-haired man whom I recognized to be the vice president, an extremely unpigmented, dead-eyed follower named Neal Shilling.

"Well done," Sill said, clapping his last couple of claps. "Nicely done. You got in. I wouldn't say undetected, but here you are. I'm impressed. You have to be careful who you trust. My spies are everywhere."

I looked at Eigen. She was awake and standing beside me, but one look at her face told me she was terrified and surprised. I turned to Karras.

The priest shrugged. "What can I fucking say?"

Eigen looked at Karras with contempt, but I felt shame that I actually imagined I had been betrayed by Eigen.

"Come on down," Sill said. "Join us for a short briefing before we move to the observatory."

I led the way down the curved stairs, Eigen right behind me, Karras lagging several steps behind.

"Thank you, Damien," Sill said, then he nodded to Gloria. "Gloria?"

Gloria raised a pistol and fired one shot. The boom filled the library. Several of the suited men jumped, as did I. Eigen latched on to my back and stayed there as I turned to see Karras flat against the stairs, his chest a wide-open red mess. Eigen screamed. The world came slowly back into focus. "What the fuck" were the last words Father Damien Karras uttered.

"What happened to the silencer?" Sill asked. "It's so much cooler with a silencer. That was just plain loud." He turned to the rest of us. "Well, still exciting, right? I didn't need him anymore. I just hate anyone who can't be trusted. I mean, I trusted him, but you couldn't. How long before I couldn't? You understand what I'm saying."

I looked at the vice president, then to Sill. "You're telling me the government's in on this?"

The VP and his Secret Service detail laughed.

"Professor Kitu, I'd like to introduce you to the vice president, Neal Shilling," Sill said. "Behind him over in the corner is Farnsworth K. Farnsworth, owner and CEO of Meganational Foods. He owns ninety percent of the world's food production. Over there is Hotswath Bajaj. Mr. Bajaj has quietly, and with a bit of my help, acquired over seventy-five percent of all pharmaceutical manufacturing on the planet. Arms maker, arms dealer, religious leader." He pointed at person after person. "Names really don't matter. Let's do this thing. To the telescope."

We were ushered down the hall to the observatory. Jean Luc Monfils was decked out in an extra-crisp white lab coat, towering over everyone. "The window is about to open," he said.

Sill stood next to the big monitor. "Adjacent to the city of Boston, Massachusetts, is a township named Quincy. I don't like it because the way the people who live there pronounce it."

"The window is opening," Monfils said.

"A lot of White racists live there," Sill said. "I could have chosen any number of places, but I was once called a nigger in Quincy. Quinzee, they say. Quinnnnzzeee. A speech defect?"

"Now," Monfils said.

I saw this as my moment. They were all watching the screen. I ran to the eyepiece of the giant telescope. I tried to focus. It took me a few seconds to realize that I was seeing nothing. I was too late.

"Too late, Wala," Sill said.

"Quincy is no more. Milton is now adjacent to Weymouth and Braintree. I love that name, Braintree. I've been there. Pure irony."

Shilling cleared his throat. "Sill, are you trying to tell me that all of those people in Quincy are dead?"

"What people?" Sill asked.

"The people in Quincy?"

"There is no Quincy. Look at the GPS on your phones."

The men did. At the same time Monfils brought up a satellite image of Massachusetts on the screen. The shape of the state was changed. Hull and Allerton at the tip of Nantasket were now nearly touching South Boston.

I felt hollow. I felt grief. I was too slow. I couldn't recognize nothing until it was too late.

"This is fantastic," Shilling said. "The power. Can you do it again? Say, to China or North Korea."

"No, we've shot our wad this time."

"You mean we wasted that on Quincy, Massachusetts?" Shilling said.

"Thanks to Professor Kitu," Sill said. "But you also have him to thank for the thing working. Before he could recognize nothing, it found its way here. If he hadn't seen it coming, nothing couldn't have happened. As it is, nothing happened and therefore nothing has changed."

"But Quincy?" Eigen asked.

"Nothing," Sill said.

"Is Quincy gone?"

"Is what gone? There is nothing there. There was always nothing there. That's the real beauty of this weapon. The resultant destruction is always already there."

Farnsworth K. Farnsworth slapped Hotswath Bajaj a high five and said, "Damn it, I don't understand it, but I love it. Don't you love it, Hotswath?"

"I love it."

"Let's go to my house and have a drink," Shilling said.

Sill signaled to his men. "Take his dog. He won't try to disappear if we have his mutt tucked away."

The larger of my attackers from the canal reached for Trigo in the bag I had set down next to Eigen's feet. I raced for it, but he got there first. He waved a finger in my face and smiled evilly.

"Gentlemen," Sill said.

I felt a sharp pain in the back of my head and the world went black.

Humpty Dumpty's extreme practice

1

It was certainly not the case that Descartes or Berkeley or Husserl would have actually considered an empirical adaptation of the relationship with the physical world or with scientific truth or the quality of an emotion as the premise of a syllogism. Berkeley would always step out of the way of the oncoming carriage. Philosophical conviction seldom leads to real-world modification. I could tell myself that the pain was merely reportage from my body that some trauma had occurred and therefore I could talk myself out of the sensation, but that was all bullshit. My head hurt like hell, even though I knew I was dreaming and not awake. I was lost in the dream without my guide. Where was my Trigo? I entered the dream with the knowledge that the house I was inside possessed the floor plan of that very house. The house was a drawing of itself, with furniture placed where the furniture would be placed in the real house, with doors that opened and closed just like the real doors of the real house. But I was in the floor plan of that house and so I assumed I was safe. I wandered through it, wondering where one might hide a dog. Many versions of reality occur at once, I was told by a quantum physicist. I just stared at him and said, "Could you repeat that? I wasn't listening."

I was wandering the floor plan of the vice president's residence at One Observatory Circle. As I passed from the pantry kitchen to the dining room, I recalled that nothing had happened to Quincy, Massachusetts. I was both relieved and horrified. Because though nothing had happened there, nothing had happened there and what was left was nothing. More than ninety thousand people were up to nothing, had gone to nothing, had been affected by nothing and were left with nothing and there was nothing to do or say. And it was not a matter of perspective. Any perspectival rendering, by logic, whim, or design, required a vector of sorts, even if static.

I called my dog's name as I passed through the rooms, or rather plans of the rooms. In the library where books had never been touched, because here they were not books but precise, one might say *exact*, if one were inclined to such speech, replicas of the actual books in the actual library, in the actual house of the actual vice president. I thought I heard Trigo whimper, but it turned out it was me, the me caught in a hall mirror as I passed. I realized that the image of me in the mirror was not me, not only because it was my reflection, but not of me because the mirror was not a real mirror but a marker for the real one that was in the real residence. And then I reasoned that if I could manage to find my actual reflection someplace in the floor plan then I could use that real reflection's connection with me, it being me, and find my way into the actual house where Trigo was being held. I sat on a sofa that wasn't a sofa in the not–sitting room, found it uncomfortable nonetheless, and wondered if I was actually in my dream or in a dream mock-up, perhaps a set of a later dream. Since I couldn't dream without Trigo, what was I in fact doing? *Nothing* haunted me as I wandered from room to room, until I found myself in the living room, near the windows that opened onto the veranda, where stood the not–vice president. The replica was different from the real thing. There was more spark of life in his eyes, though he didn't engage with me, but stood there, dusty like the unread likenesses of books from the plan of the library. I asked him where was my dog, but there was no discernible response. Beside him stood a Secret Service agent that I had not seen before, yes, *that* I had not seen before, because . . . you know. But oddness being as oddness does, this replica of an agent wore dark glasses, and as I recalled, this agent whose actual self I recalled from the observatory wore no glasses. I conveniently dream-reasoned that therefore the glasses were not replicas but actual glasses and so I looked into them for my reflection, found it, and then in turn found myself in what I knew to be the real residence. I was lying on the floor next to a sitting Eigen. We were bound, wrists behind our backs and ankles crossed, but not to each other. We were on the rough wall-to-wall carpet of one of the basement bedrooms used by the navy stewards who attended to the needs of the house. The room was dark except for some light that spilled onto us from an overhead bathroom fixture that had been left on.

"Are you okay?" Eigen asked. "Your head is bleeding."

"I think I'm all right."

"I don't know where we are," she said.

"We're in the vice president's house."

"How do you know that?"

"This is a servant's bedroom. I read a book about this house a long time ago." I looked around the room for something to cut the duct tape that secured us.

"Do you remember everything you read?"

"I don't think so, but stuff comes back. You wouldn't happen to have a knife?"

"The vice president?"

"Turns out the government is full of bad guys," I said. "Who would have thought that?"

"You're bleeding," she said, again. "They shot the priest."

"Yes."

"Killed him. I'd never seen a dead person before."

Neither had I, but I didn't think commiseration was what was needed at the moment. What was needed was a knife.

Eigen scooted on her back to the near wall and unplugged a radio that sat on the nightstand. She used the prongs of the plug to tear at the tape.

"Very smart," I said.

"Where is Trigo?" she asked as she worked on the tape.

"I don't know. I also don't know where all the people of Quincy are."

"This is horrible," she said.

It took awhile, but she managed to free her hands. Then we were both untied and standing.

"What do we do?" she asked.

"I suppose we should try to stop them from doing nothing to another town, or country even."

"I have to tell you that all this talk about nothing is confusing me," she said.

"Yes, I know." I walked to the door and put my ear to it, placed my hand on the cut-glass knob, and gave a little twist. The door was unlocked. Eigen came and stood close behind me. Peeking through a crack, I could see that the pantry to which the room opened was lit and empty.

"Where are we going?" Eigen asked.

"Suffice it to say we're not staying," I said.

Across the room we found the vertical sliding door of a dumb-waiter beside the stairs. The conveyor was open and we could hear voices.

"That's Sill," I whispered.

"Men, this is a new day. All you have to do is not be here in three days when I again harness nothing and release it. When DC is nothing, the US will be nothing and there will be nothing left to do."

"And that fat buffoon will be the nothing that he is," said Shilling. "I've hated kissing his orange ass for these past years. Stable genius? Stable asshole."

All the men laughed.

"The president has no idea?" asked Bajaj.

"He has no idea about anything," Shilling said. "I'm afraid of him because he literally knows nothing."

"But he believes he knows everything," Sill said. "And of course that's why he's nothing but a fuckup."

"Doesn't it bother you, Mr. Sill, that so many Black people will be affected?" Farnsworth asked.

"Sacrifices must be made," Sill said. "If there's one thing all this money has made me, it's White."

All the men laughed.

"White," Shilling said. "Yuk yuk yuk."

2

"Why do they laugh like that?" Eigen asked. "Yuk yuk yuk. They sound like a strange bird choir."

"I don't know," I said. "How do I sound when I laugh? Maybe it's a man thing."

"I don't know if I've ever heard you laugh."

"Oh."

"Should we kill them all?" Eigen asked.

I looked at her. "Kill them?"

"They're bad, right. They hurt people, didn't they? Killed people."

I nodded. "I wouldn't know how to kill someone," I told her.

"We could shoot them. The way they did the priest."

"We don't have a gun. Do you think you could do that?"

She sighed and fell back against the wall. "I don't know. Is there anyone who can help us?"

"Maybe Bill Clinton," I said.

"President Bill Clinton?"

"No. Some kind of government agent. He's working against Sill. I *think* he's working against Sill. I don't seem to know much of anything for certain." I looked at the stairwell. "Let's see if we can find a back door."

"What about Trigo?"

"They killed Father Karras. They just killed ninety thousand people. Well, sort of. I mean, nothing happened to them. I don't want to see you hurt."

"We can't leave without him," she said.

"You're right. Let's try to get up to the second-floor bedrooms."

The men laughed again. "To Fort Knox," Sill said.

"Hear, hear! Yuk yuk yuk."

We made our way quietly up the first flight of cigarette-smoke-infused carpeted stars. At the landing we could still hear the voices, but they were murky, indistinct; only the laughter was still clear. On the second floor we could hear nothing. We searched the rooms and did not find Trigo.

"We have to get out of here," I said. "These people are dangerous."

"Trigo," Eigen called out softly.

"He's not here. We'll get help and find him later."

Eigen followed me back down to the first floor and into the kitchen. An old Black man was arranging hors d'oeuvres on a platter. He looked at us with surprise, but without panic. He continued to work with the food while he talked. "Are you the ones they had tied up in the basement?"

"Yes," I said.

"I see you got loose."

"We did."

"You ain't got to worry. They never come into the kitchen. Heaven forbid one of them should come into the kitchen."

"Can we get out this way?" I asked.

He nodded.

"Are there guards or agents outside?"

He chuckled. "This here is the vice president's house. Nobody gives a fuck about the vice president. Y'all hungry?"

"We just want to get out."

He looked at Eigen. "What about you, baby girl? You hungry?"

Eigen didn't answer.

"Y'all need to eat." He pushed the platter toward us on the counter.

"Here. Have some. Sweet potato biscuits with smoked ham and apple butter."

We each took one and ate it.

"This is wonderful," Eigen said.

"My own recipe. You'd think one of them fat cats in there would ask me about that or tell me the food is good, but no. Motherfuckers too busy with *important* shit."

"Thanks for the food," Eigen said. "It really is good."

"Did you see them with a dog?" I asked.

He looked at my eyes for a couple of seconds. "That's your dog?"

"They took my dog," I said.

"Describe him," he said.

"He's a bulldog with one leg."

"Damn," he said.

"What?"

"He's in the washroom over there. The Secret Service brought him in and left him. He's a sweet animal. I was going to take him home with me."

Eigen went directly to the washroom.

"Thank you," I said.

"Fat face," I heard Eigen say.

"Is that his name?" the old man asked.

"His name is Trigo."

"That's a nice name."

"Don't you want to know why they had us tied up?" I asked.

"Nope. All I know is that they're the bad guys and that makes you the good guys. So take your dog and get out of here. Here, take some food with you." He grabbed some foil and started wrapping up the biscuits.

"Thank you."

"You're welcome."

Eigen came out with Trigo in her arms and the empty bag over her shoulder.

The man reached over and scratched Trigo's chin. "He's such a nice dog. How old is he?"

"He's thirteen," I told him.

The man smiled. "He's almost my age. In people years he's ninety-one and I'm ninety-two."

"And you're still working?"

"Still gotta eat," he said. "Still gotta eat."

"Thank you so much," Eigen said.

"No problem, baby girl." He stroked the top of Trigo's head. "I was gonna take him home and name him Signifier, you know, like the signifying monkey."

"That's a fine name," I said. I looked at the door to the grounds. I studied the old man's eyes and he looked back at me. His gaze let me in and I could see how sharp his mind was, how much he had seen, how much he had ignored and endured.

The yuk-yukking came from the other room. "Never trust anyone with a laugh you can spell," the old man said.

"Sounds like good advice," I said. "What is your name?"

"My name is Leon Coltrane, like the saxophone player."

"You were going to take him home with you?"

"Sure was."

I looked at Trigo and he nodded. I hoped my friend could see my sadness and my trepidation. "Will you?" I asked the man.

"Will I what?"

"Will you take Trigo home with you?"

"You're serious?"

"Yes, sir."

He beamed. "I sure will."

Eigen looked at me and put the dog in the old man's arms. He struggled a bit with the weight. He let Trigo lick his face.

"You gonna come back for him?"

I looked at Eigen and then at Trigo. "No."

"Thank you," the old man said.

"No, sir," I said. "Thank you."

Laughter erupted from the front room again.

"We're going now."

"Okay," he said. "All I know is that y'all didn't come through here."

Eigen put her hand on Coltrane's arm. "Thank you, Leon."

I nodded a goodbye to Trigo.

"Go," Trigo said.

3

To my surprise the sun was just coming up. I had lost all track of time. We sat on a bench just a couple of meters away from M Street. Eigen put a comforting hand on my back. That gesture was as surprising as the hour, showing an engagement with the moment that I had previously considered difficult for either of us.

To prove that a given set of presumptions implies a contemplated conclusion, prove that the premises are at variance with the negation of that conclusion. Logic was simple enough to employ and understand, but hard to make useful. The rules were always clear, exacting, but had little to do with reality. I sat there on the cold bench trying to reason to our next move.

"Do you have any ideas?" I asked Eigen.

"No," she said.

"Are you cold?"

"Yes." She pushed closer to me.

"Let's find a place to rest."

We crossed M Street and walked toward the waterfront. The desk clerk at the Georgetown Inn was upset that I wanted to pay cash for a room.

"I will need a credit card for incidentals," she said.

"What are incidentals?" I asked.

"Room service, movies."

"We don't want room service or movies. I want to pay cash."

"We're not set up to accept cash."

As I stood there, I thought of Bill Clinton. "Okay," I said, "I'll use my card." I gave her my debit card.

"Whew," she said. "I was afraid I wasn't going to be able to help you, Mr. Kitu."

"Two beds, please," I said.

"Of course. We do have a wonderful selection of movies."

"Terrific."

"You're lucky we have a room ready. Check-in is usually at three."

"It feels good to be lucky," I said.

"Do you need help with your bags?"

"We don't have bags," Eigen said.

"I see." She gave us the key cards and we walked to the elevators.

"Why did you change your mind about the credit card?" Eigen asked.

"I'm trying to send a signal to Bill Clinton."

4

I lay on the bed nearer the window while Eigen stepped into the shower. Neither of us had uttered Trigo's name. I felt that I had done the correct and right thing. I believed he was safe with Leon Coltrane and that Leon Coltrane was safe with him. I closed my eyes and wondered who would advise me in my dreams.

Th square root of two is not a rational number, so says the theorem. The proof is rationally boring, as proofs go. The theorem does not prove that the square root of two is a real number. The beauty of this was in the reaction of the Pythagoreans who discovered it—shock. I loved the notion that anyone would be so moved by a bit of number theory. Shocked. In my dream I had wandered into a truck stop at a typical freeway exit called Metempsychosis. Truck drivers ate chili and drank beer and watched other trucks roll by on the dark highway outside.

Eigen was a waitress. She stopped at a booth and spoke to four truckers. "What in the h-e-l-l do you want?"

"How is the pie?" asked a man.

"Calculated to fifty places," she said.

"I'll have the square root of two," another man said.

"Oh, come on," Eigen said. "Let us assume that the square root of two is rational. That means that there exist integers p and q such that . . ." She gave them the proof. "Since 2\1 is false, so is our assumption that the square root of two is a rational number."

"So, I should have the chili?" the man asked.

"Good call," she said.

Suddenly I was aware of myself at the counter observing the interaction. Eigen saw me looking at her and walked over, asked me what in the h-e-l-l I wanted.

"I want to know what to do next," I said.

"Don't we all?"

"What is your name?" I asked.

"Oh, names don't matter," she said. "Is my name really *my* name? There are lots of people with my name. Let's say my name is Mary. Can we say that?"

"Yes."

"But Mary is the name of my name, but I am not my name. My name and I are not interchangeable. So, though my name is Mary, I am not Mary, but it's what you call me, if you choose to call me. Do you choose to call me? What is your name?"

"Humpty," I said.

"Now that's a name," she said. "It doesn't rhyme with many things, does it. Except for"—she opened the menu on the counter in front of me and pointed at item thirty-seven—"Dumpty."

"Dumpty?"

"Dumpty. Made fresh every day."

"Is it good?" I asked.

"No, it's terrible, but it is number thirty-seven on the menu and that counts for something."

"Why is that?"

"Thirty-seven is an odd number, silly."

"So are two, three, five, seven, eleven, thirteen, seventeen, twenty-three, twenty-nine, thirty-one, forty-one, forty-three, and forty-seven," I said.

"Yes, but thirty-seven is special."

"Why?"

"Because if you turn it around, it's still prime. Seventy-three."

"But that's true of thirteen and seventeen, also."

"Then you should have the chili."

"What's that have to do with anything?"

"Are we going to Fort Knox? Wala?"

"What?"

"Wala?"

I woke up. "Yes?"

"Are we going to Fort Knox?" Eigen asked. She was sitting next to me on the bed.

"Do you think we should?" I asked.

There was a knock at the door and then a crash at the window. Armored men came through the big window attached to ropes. Weapons at the ready. Then the door was kicked in by more soldiery types. They surrounded Eigen and me.

5

Mitchell walked in first. His black suit was pressed and stiff, as was he. He was followed by the somewhat less impressive looking Bill Clinton. His suit was olive khaki, an army green that might have looked good on a soldier, but probably not. It was Clinton who spoke first.

"I told you that you couldn't hide from us."

"When did you tell me that?" I asked.

"Didn't I tell him that?" he asked Mitchell.

Mitchell shrugged.

"I'm certain I said that to you." He pointed his finger at me. "So forget about running."

"What happened in Massachusetts?" I asked.

"What are you talking about?" Clinton and Mitchell sat on the other bed and faced Eigen and me.

"Why didn't you just knock?" Eigen asked.

"We did," Mitchell said.

"But then you came through the window," she said.

"Your point?" Mitchell asked.

"Never mind that," Clinton said. "What about Massachusetts?"

"Quincy," I said. "How are things in Quincy?"

"What's Quincy?"

"The town of Quincy."

Clinton looked at Mitchell and Mitchell looked at his phone. "Looking it up," Mitchell said.

"It's right next to Boston. Not right next to it. It's next to Braintree."

"I know Braintree," Clinton said.

"There is no Quincy," Mitchell said.

"What are you saying?" I asked Mitchell.

"I'm saying there is no Quincy, Massachusetts. What are *you* saying?"

"There was a Quincy. Ninety thousand people. Sill erased it."

Clinton and Mitchell looked at each other, then Clinton stared at my eyes. "Are you all right?"

"There was a Quincy," Eigen said.

"There *was* a Quincy," Clinton said. "A whole town existed that we didn't know about?" Mitchell waved his phone in our faces.

"It was right there," I said, pointing at the little screen. "The bay used to be much wider."

The men laughed. They sounded alarmingly similar to Sill, the vice president, and their group. Yuk yuk yuk.

"I'm telling you there used to be a Quincy, Massachusetts," I said.

"Sill disappears a whole town and its population?" Clinton shook his head.

"Drugs," Mitchell said.

"You said you wanted to know what Sill was up to. Well, I'm telling you. They did nothing to Quincy."

"Which would be really easy since there is no Quincy to do anything to. Did Sill put you up to this?"

"Where's your dog?" Mitchell asked. "He disappear, too?"

"As a matter of fact."

"Do you smell lilacs?" Mitchell asked.

Clinton sniffed. "I do."

Begriff und Gegenstand

1

Gottlob Frege was drinking tea. Though we were sitting at the same small table in a little café, he was turned away. I knew he was a shy man, so I said nothing.

"You know, if it weren't for Bertrand Russell, my ideas would have been lost," Frege said.

"And Peano," I said.

"Yes, him, also." He looked at me. You're not drinking your tea. Don't you like it?"

"I don't know," I said. "I haven't tasted it." I sniffed the tea. "Lilac."

I awoke to find Gloria sitting directly in front of me. From the seats I knew we were on Sill's jet. I looked over to see Eigen asleep beside me. Gloria might have smiled at me, but she certainly stared at me. Somehow her gaze did not go right through me but stopped just inches in front of me. Her afro was back. I looked out the window at the darkness.

"Why aren't you flying the plane?" I asked.

"Autopilot."

"You mean there's no one at the controls?"

"I didn't say that. I said autopilot."

"So you did."

Since I had just awakened, I expected Eigen to as well, but she remained asleep, moving a little to get comfortable.

"She is okay," Gloria said.

"So, what's your story? Where did you learn to fly? Were you in the military? Did you start with a broom?"

"No. I was pro—" She stopped as Eigen moved again. "I learned when I was young. My father was a pilot."

"What did your father do?"

"He taught me to fly."

"I mean for work. What was his job?"

"Business. He was in business."

"You said before he was a dry cleaner."

"Did I?"

We encountered a bit of rough air. I watched as nothing registered on her face. "Are you on medication?" I realized as I said it that my blurting that out was inappropriate, perhaps rude, but it didn't faze her.

"No," she said.

"Can you tell me where we're going?" I asked.

"Yes."

"Will you?"

"We're on our way to Kentucky."

"Fort Knox?"

"Kentucky. Mr. Sill's cabin. It is near Elizabethtown."

"I see."

"Would you like to have sex?"

"No, thank you." I studied Gloria's face. "How did we get here? The last thing I remember was talking to the government agents. Did you kill them?"

"No."

"How did you find us?"

"We followed Bill Clinton and he led us to you."

"I see. Lilacs?"

"Sleeping gas."

Eigen stirred. This time she was actually waking up. She stretched and looked at me. "Where are we?" she asked.

"On a plane," I said. This time that answer did actually impart information. "This is Gloria."

Eigen eyed her suspiciously, perhaps recognizing her. "Is this Sill's plane? Gloria? Is she dangerous?" Her voice grew softer with each question. "Where are we going?" A mere whisper now.

"Kentucky."

She sat back and looked at the empty seat in front of her. "I've never been to Kentucky."

"Neither have I," I said.

"What's there?"

"Nothing. A lot of nothing."

"Do you work for Sill?" Eigen asked.

"I do."

"Does he pay you a lot of money or do you believe in what he believes in?" Eigen sounded confident.

Gloria tilted her head and observed Eigen.

"Is he your leader?" Eigen asked.

"My leader," Gloria repeated. She was incredulous.

Eigen looked at me, frustrated.

"Does Sill plan to kill us?" I asked.

"Yes."

I could see the fear on Eigen's face.

"Shouldn't you get back to flying the plane?" I asked.

Gloria nodded. "Yes."

She got up and walked toward the flight deck. Eigen grabbed my arm and squeezed. "I'm scared," she said.

"Sill needs me," I told her. "He's not going to hurt us."

"Not until he gets what he wants."

"He'll never get it."

The door closed behind Gloria.

"She's so strange," Eigen said.

I nodded. "Obviously there's no way off this plane, so I'll tell you what I know. It's not much. Sill believes that there is nothing in the bullion depository."

"What does he think is in there?"

"Nothing."

"Nothing?"

"Absolutely nothing."

"I don't understand."

"He wants me to devise a way to keep nothing nothing. Somehow he managed to use it for a split second to do what he did to Quincy."

"To what?"

"Quincy."

She stared at me.

"Quincy, Massachusetts."

Eigen shook her head, not understanding.

I, however, was beginning to understand. Quincy did not exist, and if it did not exist, then it had never existed. The only thing that can yield nothing is nothing. Quincy was always nothing because now it was nothing. What made me uneasy was that I believed that I had had some part in nothing happening. If I hadn't been there, nothing never could have happened and there would still be a Quincy. But now, somehow because of me, there had never been a Quincy. Earth now lacked some twenty-seven square miles but was still no different, since nothing had happened.

"How are you supposed to control nothing?" Eigen asked.

"I don't know. But I know nothing and this is not going to be easy. My fear is that anything can happen."

"But nothing will, right?"

I looked at her and nodded.

"What's the story with Gloria?" she asked.

"What do you mean?"

"She seems especially focused on you. She didn't appear concerned with me at all. I'm not even sure she saw me."

"I think she's crazy. She keeps asking me if I want to have sex."

"Oh."

"I find it an odd question. It's the *have* I don't get. Does one have it? Or perform it? Do it? I've heard that. People don't have tennis."

"People have surgery," she said.

"That's true. One doesn't have a test. One takes a test."

"Do you think you should have sex with her?"

"Do you think that might benefit us?" I asked.

"I don't know."

We sat quietly for a while. The plane hit another patch of turbulence.

"What should we do?" Eigen asked.

"Let's think."

And that's what we did.

2

The most common of speakers of any language are capable of using nearly any word in a wide range of contexts and situations, employing varying meanings, with complete ownership, and can be understood. There is perhaps no confusion as profound as when one's utterance means nothing to those who hear it. As when I say, "The world will never be the same because nothing is happening to it." Nothing is changing. I say that now and it terrifies me. It was the fact that nothing never changed; but now that nothing has happened, nothing will never be the same. The distinction between negation and nothing is no small concern. What is the theater expression? There are no small concerns, only small concepts. Something like that. I had a colleague say to me of his ex-spouse, "I feel nothing for her." To which I responded, "You should let her feel that for herself." He thought I was brilliant, bragged me up and down as a genius regarding relationships. Later, he asked me how I had come to be so wise and I said, "Because nothing matters." He thought I was being dismissive and walked away. Nothing matters.

The jet touched down early in the foggy morning. It seemed we were always landing in the morning. The landing strip here was private and adjacent to Sill's Kentucky residence. I was fairly certain that there was no other home like it in Kentucky as we were driven toward it in a red Jeep. Gloria drove. I thought this person could drive anything. Cars, planes, submarines.

Eigen was frightened, but not more than I was. We held hands. That was new; however, it did feel strange or foreign.

The house was glass and steel, sprawling and yet somehow incorporated into the landscape. It didn't look as if it had been built but instead had appeared, in spite of the materials and hard edges, to have grown there.

Sill stepped out to greet us. He applauded. "We're going to have to stop meeting like this. Hello, Eigen."

His voice obviously affected her significantly. Her grip on my hand tightened briefly, then melted.

"Where is your dog?" he asked.

"I don't know," I said.

I knew that he knew I was lying. "No matter," he said. "It's difficult to keep up with a dog that can't keep up. I think that's an old saying. If it's not, it should be. We should put together a book of wise old sayings. We could call it the Book of Wise Old Sayings. Or the Bible."

We stood awkwardly for a few seconds.

"Come on in. Let's have a snack. Something to tide us over until lunch. Maybe you'd like to freshen up."

DeMarcus was waiting just inside the house. "Sir," he greeted me. I could tell he was looking for Trigo, but he said nothing about him. "I will show you to your rooms."

"Go ahead," Sill said. "Run along." He waved. "Get cleaned up and then meet me in the library. You'll find it. This house has the exact same floor plan as the house in Miami. Of course, the view from your rooms will be different. No blue water, just bluegrass."

Gloria escorted Eigen away and I was asked to follow DeMarcus. He delivered me to a room that was not the same as, but not unlike, the room I had occupied in Miami.

"How are you?" I asked.

"Very well, sir."

"DeMarcus, do you know what your employer does?"

"It is not my place to know."

"But do you?"

The tall man looked at me for a long second, collected himself, and said, "No."

"You asked about my dog," I said.

Again, a look.

"Mr. Sill had him killed." I said this and studied the man's eyes.

There was a change inside him. His shoulders sagged a centimeter. "Will that be all for now, sir?"

"Yes."

DeMarcus closed the door. I walked to the window and looked out at an expanse of pasture dotted with black and bay horses. The fog had lifted. I felt bad about the lie I had told DeMarcus, but I found myself needing to know who around me was human and complete with feelings. I was terrified that Eigen was venturing again down that hypnotic path she was on before.

I went to the door and found it unlocked.

3

The route through the house to the library was so familiar as to be eerie. Not because it was dreamlike, but because it was mundane. Instead of marble the floors here were hardwood and no matter how hard I tried I could not make my footsteps silent. I had no idea why I wanted to erase my sound, but I did want to and I tried. It turned out that the library was not as grand as the one in Miami, actually a pleasing feature. It was warmer. I had little interest in looking at the collection. The glass wall looked out onto a short meadow of flowers and a forest beyond, hills beyond that. I sat on a rattan davenport with flowered cushions and stared at the stand of trees.

"I thought I might find you here." It was Sill. He sat on the davenport with me. "Those are mostly black oaks and sourwood. I think trees are like people."

"How is that?"

"Each one is unique. No oak is exactly like any other oak. They stand in plain view, but what feeds them is hidden from view. And even though they can be old and sturdy, a stiff wind can upset them, rip them from the world they know. That can happen to us, can't it? Somehow we endure it better. Do you know much about plants?"

"Some."

"What about angiosperms?" he asked.

"Angiospermae are seed-producing land plants, sixty-four orders, four hundred and sixteen families, thirteen thousand genera, and three hundred thousand species."

Sill chuckled.

"What is it?"

"This is why I need you around. You amuse me."

"I'm glad you find me amusing. Where is Eigen?" I asked.

"She's fine. She's very much like you. All nerdy and Aspergery and awkward and brilliant."

"How do you plan to get into the bullion depository?"

"Details, details. You needn't worry your pretty little head over the details. Just sweat the big stuff. I need you to concern yourself with nothing and nothing else."

"What's all the villain stuff about anyway?" I asked.

"You won't believe this, but no one has ever asked me that question."

"You're a billionaire. You don't need money. You can go where you want, do what you want."

"I just want to get even," he said.

"Even? With whom?"

"America, Wala. America."

"This is about race?"

"No, this is about exacting payment, or, should I say, repayment."

"For what?"

"This is a rather boring conversation. Don't you have something cool to say about infinity or zero or imaginary numbers? Tell me something that makes no sense. That's why I hired you."

We sat there for a minute.

"I'm waiting," he said.

"I don't understand why language allows me to actually say something sensical that is not true."

Sill sighed. "I was hoping for something better than that. Try again. Please."

"Even though we know that pi and *e* are transcendental, we don't know whether the sum of pi and *e* is transcendental or algebraic."

"See, that's more like it." Sill leaned forward and put his elbows on his knees. "What should we do now? Badminton?"

I said nothing.

"I was just joking. I hate badminton. I hate all racquet sports." He stood. "Let's go see Eigen."

I stood up.

"You've changed, Wala."

"How so?" I asked.

"I don't know. You're just different. Maybe you're taller."

"I'm not taller."

"Then maybe I'm shorter." He looked at me. "Perhaps it's the case that the whole world is smaller."

"Then I would be taller."

"That's right, isn't it?"

He led us through the house and out the opposite side. We marched toward a couple of rust-colored buildings set on a knoll. The structures turned out to be stables, clean, manicured. Eigen was standing just inside one of them, rubbing the nose of a beautiful gray horse.

"Oh, Wala, isn't she gorgeous?" she said.

The haltered animal was being held on a lead rope by Gloria. She might have smiled at me. I stood next to Eigen and stroked the horse's neck.

"Isn't she something?" Eigen said. "Her name is Lilac a Rug. Do you get it? Her mother was Lilac Perfume and her father was Cut a Rug."

"Nice," I said. "Eigen, are you all right?"

She didn't seem to hear my question. At least she didn't respond.

"She'll be my entry in the Derby," Sill said. "She stands a good chance. She actually enjoys being pushed. What about you, Wala? Do you enjoy being pushed?"

"Not particularly," I said.

"What about you, Eigen?"

"What?" she asked.

"Do you like to be pushed?"

"I don't know what you mean," she said.

Sill pulled some strands of hair from her face and gently pushed them behind her ear. "How are you feeling, darling?"

"I'm wonderful," Eigen said. She looked right at me. "I'm wonderful."

"Yes, you are," said Sill. Sill looked at my eyes. "Yes, she is."

4

We were seated at Sill's customarily well-appointed lunch table on a lawn just below the pool and once again we were joined by General Takitall. This time, however, the general was not in uniform but dressed in a Hawaiian shirt, Bermuda shorts, and orange Crocs on his surprisingly small feet.

"Professor Kitu, we meet again," Takitall said. "Look at this lunch. John, you've outdone yourself."

"Lunch is, without doubt, the most important meal of the day," Sill said. "Isn't that right, Eigen?"

"I love lunch," Eigen said.

I looked at the table.

"DeMarcus, run down the menu for us," Sill said.

DeMarcus cleared his throat. He pointed. "Here we have Guinness-poached lobster with dill smetana, wild trout roe, and fennel flowers. Here we have cubes of marble rye bread stuffed with caramelized onions and Parmesan custard. Finally, masa toro topped with Marky's Imperial Beluga Hybrid caviar."

"I don't care about your fucking expensive and fancy foods," I said. "I'll have a roast beef sandwich. A damn pizza. And not one with edible gold on it."

"Looks to me like somebody got up on the wrong side of the quadrilateral," Takitall said.

"Eigen!" I shouted. "What the hell is wrong with you?" I fell exhausted back into my chair.

"Are we done?" Sill asked me.

I nodded.

"Very good, the rest of us will now enjoy the, as you called it, expensive and fancy food."

"Excuse me," I said. "I believe I'll return to my room."

"Gloria, see that the professor doesn't get lost."

"Of course, Mr. Sill," Gloria said. "Professor."

I looked at Eigen one long, last time and then got up and left the table, Gloria on my heels.

"You realize I know the way," I said.

"Yes," she said.

"What is Sill doing to my friend?"

"Nothing that she is not receptive to."

"What does that mean?" I asked. "Aside from the fact that you use questionable grammar?"

"Was that an attempt at insult?"

"Apparently not a successful one. Gloria, I have three million dollars in the bank. Would you like it?"

"I'm sure I would."

"Do you want it?"

"Who would not?"

"May I offer it to you?"

"That, of course, is up to you."

At the door of my room, I turned to face her. "I will give you all of my money if you help me get Eigen away from Sill."

"No."

"I will give you the money if you tell me how I can get her away from him," I said. "Just information. That's it."

"I suggest you get a gun and shoot him," she said. She might have smiled, it was hard to tell. It was clear I was getting nowhere. "Are you going to lock me in here?"

"No."

"Are you going to stand outside my door?"

"Yes."

I stepped inside and closed the door myself. I walked to the window and looked at the horses. Even if I did get out of my room undetected, what could or would I do? If I could get out, how would I help Eigen? I didn't know how to do anything. It occurred to me that that might have been the story of my life. Whether it was or not, I believed that it didn't have to be, adhering, as I did, to the notion that contingency is necessary.

I lay on the bed and tried to dream and conjure a conversation with Trigo. My mind began to race and play tricks. Every effort to conjure my friend resulted in a different breed. Trigo as a Labrador retriever tried to get me to taste his food and got angry when I wouldn't. Trigo would have said, Suit yourself. Trigo as a Rottweiler asked me if I knew the difference between a rabbit and a hare. When I said I didn't, he said neither did he. As a Chihuahua he refused to speak at all. As a standard poodle, he wouldn't shut up, speaking in German, reminding me constantly that he was a hunting dog. Finally there was no dog, but ninety-two-year-old Leon Coltrane.

"I want you to know," Coltrane said, "that I have a good ten years left and so I will outlive Signifier. Yes, I changed his name. I hope you don't mind."

"I don't," I said.

"You're in quite the predicament."

I nodded.

"Where I grew up we'd say you were fucked. Pardon my French." He was dressed as a chef, but his hat was hard like a helmet. "Do you have a plan? Not that a plan is the best thing to have always."

"Do you mean I should just wing it?"

"Hope ain't no kind of strategy. You need to give them what

they want. You need to give them everything they want. You need to let them believe that you don't want them to have what they want."

"You're saying I should give them nothing?"

"As much of it as you can get."

"Just let them have it. Just like that?"

"As much as possible. It's nothing to you."

"What about Eigen?" I asked.

"Eigen will be Eigen. You have to trust her." Coltrane looked at his hands. "A little about me. My last name is Coltrane but we're no relation. I think we'd be about the same age. I mention him, though, because of time. Time is like nothing. Everybody keeps it, but nobody knows where. It's always lost or lost track of or standing still when it's not flying by. You know, that's all music is. Time. Time to recognize related tones, time to rest, to repeat, reminding us that all movement is mere illusion. There can be times on top of times, while one time slows down, another one speeds up, another stops, but they end up together as if no time has passed at all."

"You're more poetic than Trigo," I said.

"What's wonderful and something one never experiences is a song, that wonderful illusion of movement, ending on a rest."

"If it did," I said, "what difference would it make?"

"None," Coltrane said.

I asked, "If one didn't observe the rest, what would you hear differently?"

"Nothing."

"Nothing," I repeated.

"But of course it would be a different song."

He studied me while I thought about that.

"What about Sill?" I asked.

"What about him?"

"He's a villain," I said.

"So? That doesn't make him wrong. Vengeance is mine, the Lord supposedly said. I think God is big enough to share."

"I was there when he had two men killed," I said.

"Yes, that's kind of difficult to explain away. It happens? You know what I think? I think as soon as you identify a monster, it's neutered. As soon as you name it, it's done. That's what I think."

"Did you just change the subject?"

"Why would you think that? Remember that there is a distinction to be made between the future and what is to come."

"What is the difference?"

"Hell if I know."

5

I awoke from my rest thinking about the town of Quincy. Certainly the map was different, adjusted, that was there to see, sight being the privileged of our twenty-odd senses, but what must have been most affecting was the sound of nothing. Very much like a vacuum, but not, because nature abhors a vacuum; however, nature actually needs nothing. Yet nothing loves a vacuum.

It was one in the morning and a full moon had claimed the pasture. I had slept well. I couldn't imagine that Gloria had stood outside for so many hours, but when I opened the door a crack, there she was, stiff-backed and eyes forward. She didn't turn at the sound of my door, but I suspected she would have pounced had I exited and there was no telling what she would have done to me. Though she must have weighed all of 110 pounds, I had no doubt that she could beat me to a pulp without breaking a sweat. Many attendant thoughts came with a realization like that, the most disturbing being that I might have enjoyed such a thrashing. Perhaps as much as I enjoyed using the word *thrashing*.

There was a knock at my door. It was General Auric Takitall.

"Surprise," he said. "Bet you didn't expect to see me."

"That's true."

"Mind if I sit?"

"Please. Is my guard still out there?"

"Yup." He looked back at the door. "Frankly, she scares me a bit. Who am I kidding? She scares me a lot."

"I'm afraid she's going to kill me," I said.

"And then adjust her makeup."

"Or have sex with me."

He tilted his head. "Semantics."

"Why are you here?" I asked.

"Scoping things out. Getting the lay of the land. Seeing if you're a butter-side-up or a butter-side-down sort of a guy."

"Why does Sill want nothing?"

"You see, that's the problem. No one wants nothing. Sill, like the rest of us, wants something. And that's why he needs you. You believe in nothing, want nothing, want nothing from nothing. You don't turn nothing into something."

"So it's my fault nothing happened to Quincy, Massachusetts."

"Let's face it. There was pretty much nothing there to start with, but yes."

I sat on the bed.

"Don't worry, Professor. You, more than anyone, realize that nothing happened."

"What is the something that Sill wants?"

"He wants nothing to happen to this country."

"You're a general in this country's army. What are you getting out of this?"

"Forty-seven million dollars and a villa in Tuscany."

"Odd figure."

"I asked for fifty, he offered forty-five, you know how it goes."

"It's just money, then, for you."

"What money buys," he said.

"And what's that?"

"Mostly more money."

"So, I take it you don't care about this country, the people in it?"

"Fuck no. Besides, if this works, nothing will happen to anybody.

233

Everybody. I learned that from reading your papers. If you add nothing to something, what happens? Nothing. If you multiply something by nothing, what happens? Nothing. Any function with nothing will result in nothing happening. And of course nothing is not zero. Or as you've pointed out, zero is not nothing."

"Why are you here?" I asked.

"You can see that we need you. I just want you to know that."

"I don't care about money."

Takitall laughed. "Yeah, right."

"No, really," I said.

"Have it your way. But you see I do. And I'm ruthless. I have no qualms about threatening to kill your friend if you refuse to help. More importantly, I have no qualms about actually killing her. Anybody can *threaten* to kill someone."

"Just how much is a lie worth?"

"Five hundred and fifteen thousand dollars."

I stared at him.

"Well, you asked." He stood, looked at the horses. "Beautiful animals, don't you think? And know this—if I don't kill to get what I want, you can be assured that Sill will. Are we good here?" He put a hand on my shoulder, gave it a tap. "I've enjoyed our little talk, but I've got to run."

I said nothing as he walked to the door.

"Professor."

"Yes?"

"We're not bad men."

"Sill told me he's a villain."

"Oh, that. That's just a game he plays. He's really a very nice guy. If you don't believe me, ask your Rottweiler out there."

"I'll be sure to do that."

"You should know I wouldn't mind killing you, also."

"Noted."

He stared at me for a beat. "You don't rattle, do you?"

"I don't know what that means."

He nodded.

"Professor, think of it this way. This country has never given anything to us and it never will. We have given everything to it. I think it's time we gave nothing back. What do you think?"

"I'm a mathematician."

"That's what I'm counting on. Get it?" With that rather lame pun that I didn't actually *get*, as he put it, he left.

Biblical proportions and the fifth postulate

1

If space is curved, no matter how slightly, does it curve in one direction or in many, considering gravitational pulls from this source and that and this again and can it curve through so much space that it finally comes back on itself? Blah, blah, blah. Light bends and gets sucked into a black hole. Does it cease to be light? Does it fill up an ocean of light? Blah, blah, yak. For all the stars we can't count and for all the life that we argue must exist (because how can we be alone?), perhaps parallel to us, perhaps not, there is still nothing out there and that's the truth that lets us sleep at night.

I heard helicopters. Men in black armor appeared in the pasture outside my window, armed with futuristic-looking rifles, walking, trotting, running. Things were ramping up. I sat and watched for more than an hour. They were like ants but seemed to have no purpose. They carried nothing but their guns and all they did was run back and forth. There were either a few or many. How could I know as they were masked and hooded?

I reviewed all of my plans and they were perfect. I was trying to find some comfort in even a vacuous truth. I had no plans. So, conversely, I reviewed all of my plans and they were bad. Also vacuously true. All of my weapons were loaded. All of my allies were ready. None of my proofs of the fifth postulate were invalid. Truth after truth, albeit vacuous. And they did me no good. I needed to get past Gloria. I decided to try talking to her.

I opened the door. "Gloria, would you step in here?"

She did.

"Have a seat."

She did.

"Will you help me?" I asked.

"Help you what?"

"Will you help me get my friend out of here? Eigen."

"Why do you want to get her out of here? Are you in love with her?"

"No. She's my friend."

"Can you not love a friend? Would you like to have sex? I'm very good at it."

"I'm afraid I'm not," I said.

"It's a very simple procedure," she said.

Procedure was the word she used. I looked closely at her eyes that were looking at me. I had a hunch. "Do you think our apparatuses are compatible?"

"Wouldn't they have to be?"

"Do you like riddles?" I asked.

"Yes."

"Imagine this," I said. "There are three sheepherders who come to a bridge controlled by a troll and his two sons. He demands of them thirty sheep before they can pass. Each shepherd cuts out ten sheep from his flock and they give them to the troll. Once they have crossed, the troll decides that he should only have asked for twenty-five. He sends his sons after the men with five sheep. The sons decide to keep one sheep each and give three back to the herders. They do. Now it is the case that each shepherd has paid only nine sheep. Nine times three is twenty-seven. The troll sons kept two. Twenty-seven plus two is twenty-nine. Where is the missing sheep?"

Gloria's head tilted, her eyes fixed on nothing in particular, a muted hum came from her mouth. I waved my hand in front of her face and she neither acknowledged my action nor blinked. Gloria was a robot.

I left her, it, sitting on the bed and found my way to the library. I didn't know why I was headed there, but I knew where it was. From there I would begin my search for Eigen. When I arrived at the library, the sounds of helicopters had ceased. When I looked outside, I saw no mercenaries moving.

I wandered about the large room and I had the feeling someone was watching me. It being Sill's house, I had no doubt that there were cameras everywhere. But this felt different. I could almost smell someone in the room with me.

"Psssst." It was Bill Clinton. He was on the floor behind a low shelf filled with Beat poetry. He was dressed in black like the men outside. His partner, Mitchell, was lying on the floor beside him. Mitchell appeared to be reading a text on his phone.

"How did you get in here?" I asked.

"Don't look at me. Pretend to read the Ferlinghetti."

I picked up a volume of poems and pretended to read. But with the book open I couldn't help but read and so instead of pretending to read to fool the cameras, I was pretending to pretend to read to satisfy Clinton.

"Good," Clinton said. "What have you found out?"

"You ask that as if we're working together," I said.

"Well, aren't we?" Clinton asked.

Mitchell put his phone away. "Women," he said. "She thinks I ought to be there because her mother is visiting." He looked at me. "Professor. Ready to save the world?" He pulled out his pistol, pulled back the slide, and peeked in the chamber. "Ready to rock and roll?"

I looked at Clinton. "Too many movies," he said.

"I know nothing," I said.

"Yeah, we get that," Clinton said. "That's supposedly why you're here, but it doesn't make a damn bit of sense to me."

"How did you find this place?"

"A palace in the backwoods of Kentucky?"

I nodded. "Sill is not subtle."

"Anything but. It has not gone unnoticed that we are very close to Fort Knox. Is he after the gold?"

"No," I said.

"What is he after?"

"Nothing."

"I knew he was going to say that," Clinton said to Mitchell.

"Then why did you ask?" I said, looking at him.

"Look at the book," he said.

"You don't really believe Sill doesn't know you're here," I said.

"Let's assume he doesn't."

"And that there is a square root of negative two," I said. "So what do you want me to do?"

"Play along."

"Right."

"When the time comes, we'll be there and we'll make our move."

"Right."

"Is he being sarcastic?" Mitchell asked.

"More sardonic," I said.

"What? Is there a difference?" Mitchell looked at Clinton. "Can I just shoot this motherfucker?"

Clinton ignored the question.

Mitchell still looked for an answer.

"He's assuming your question was facetious," I said. "Which is slightly different from *rhetorical*."

"Just once," Mitchell said.

"Shut up," Clinton snapped.

"He said that in earnest," I said.

"We'll be close," Clinton said.

"Right," I said. "Do you know where Eigen Vector is?"

"No," he said, confirming my belief that he was useless.

"I'm going now," I said.

"Just play along."

I didn't say anything else, just walked away. At the door DeMarcus met me with a tray and glass of water. "Professor, are you quite all right?"

"That's not clear yet," I said.

"Your friend is on the second floor on the east side of the house at the end of the hall before the stairs."

"Why are you telling me this?" I asked.

"Because you want to know."

I wanted to ask him many questions, not the least of which was why he was offering assistance. I felt again suddenly bad about having lied to him about Sill killing Trigo. "DeMarcus, I have to tell you something."

"Yes?"

"Sill did not have Trigo killed. I left him with someone I trust."

A smile flashed across the man's face and then was gone.

"I'm sorry I lied to you."

He shook his head, dismissing my apology. "Mr. Sill would have gotten around to it eventually. He's very thorough."

"Eigen and me?"

He nodded. "And perhaps me." He put down the tray. "May I show you something?"

I followed DeMarcus to a nearby closet. He opened the door and there was General Takitall lying on the floor.

"What's wrong with him?" I asked.

"Everything."

"You mean he's dead."

"Precisely that."

"Sill?"

"Who else?"

"There are two government agents here," I said.

DeMarcus didn't seem surprised by the information, but he

did say, "I was unaware of their presence. I suppose they could be responsible."

"But you doubt it," I said.

"I doubt it," he repeated.

"Thank you for your help," I said.

He nodded, pulled shut the closet door.

2

I went back to the library believing for some reason that Clinton and Mitchell should be made aware of General Takitall's newly acquired condition, but they had disappeared into the woodwork. I attempted to orient myself so as to ascertain which direction was east, a not-so-easy task as I felt more than a little dizzy. I managed to find a staircase and climbed. It was not at all difficult to move quietly over the carpeted floor, but it occurred to me that my stealth was wasted, as I was positive that I was being observed on one of a battery of monitors on a wall in some well-appointed security office manned, as it were, by a battery of Glorias, each with her own battery.

As it turned out the stairs led to the middle of a corridor and so there were four doors at the top. I chose a door, stood outside, and held the knob. I listened, trying to hear any movement at all. I took a deep breath, turned the knob, and entered. It was not a bedroom at all. It was a conference room, a war room like ones I had seen in movies, admirals pushing tiny ship models around on a vast blue nautical chart. But this table was not a chart of the ocean or a mere map of the land but a model of Fort Knox and the US Bullion Depository. The detail was amazing, buildings, trees, bushes, soldiers, and even potholes in roads. There were lavender-colored letters on top of the depository that read *Operation Lilac*. There was so much detail that I found myself looking for myself, for Sill, for Eigen. I remembered that I was in fact only looking for Eigen and decided to move on to the next room.

In the next room I found Eigen, but sitting with her, waiting for me, was John Sill. "Well, it took you long enough. How can this operation go like clockwork if one of my principals is running on BPT?"

"Sorry." I looked at Eigen. I could see that she was still in a trance or drugged, I didn't know which, but I could also see fear in her eyes.

"What held you up?"

"Do you know that your general friend is dead?"

"I didn't know that," he said. "That's an alarming bit of news."

"And yet you don't appear alarmed."

"It serves no one to get excited about anything. Don't you think it's better to remain calm?"

"Like Eigen here?" I asked.

"There's calm and then there's—" He stopped.

"Drugged?" I said.

Sill shrugged.

"Are you telling me you're not responsible for the general's death?"

"Yep."

"Then who did it?"

He shrugged again. "Villainy is messy, unpredictable, erratic, fickle, one might even say inconstant. How would a mathematician put it?"

"Unpredictable is good."

"I was thinking you might suggest *variable*. At any rate, no one lives forever. There once was a general from Trent, whose dick was crooked and bent, it caused him much trouble so he put it in double and instead of coming he went."

"Takitall was from Trent?" I asked.

"No, I just like limericks. I mean, who doesn't?"

"I don't," Eigen said.

Sill and I looked at her.

"I like sonnets. And villanelles."

"Eigen and I will be leaving now," I said. Nothing sounds like a lack of confidence like one's trying to sound confident.

"You can't go now. Your departure is not a scripted part of Operation Lilac." A couple of Sill's large, formerly Sikh, men stepped into the room from the hallway. "You see, you really must come with us. It will be like nothing you've seen before." Then to his henchmen, "Bring them. And be careful with the male." He laughed. "We want to be certain that nothing happens to him." He leaned close to me. "Literally."

The men dragged us behind him down the stairs.

Sill continued to talk. "*Literally.* Don't you just hate it when people use that word? I mean, I literally hate it. Hate it, hate it, hate it. I want to kill those people. Figuratively. Who am I kidding? Literally."

We exited the house and stood before a parked line of open military jeeps. "I know what you're thinking," Sill said. "Are we there yet? Nope."

The henchmen sat with Eigen in the back of the lead jeep. I was in the passenger seat and Sill drove. He drove the manual transmission rather expertly; I admired that.

"I take it we're headed to Fort Knox."

"Correct."

"I hear it's rather heavily guarded," I said.

"Yes, well, guards are only effective if they are awake." One of his men pushed gas masks toward us from the rear. "Put it on," Sill said.

I looked back to see that a mask had already been placed over Eigen's face. I put it on. It was heavy and smelled of pine disinfectant.

"Sorry about the smell." Sill's muffled voice came to me through his mask. "At least you know it's clean. That's a good thing, right?" Inside his mask he whistled "Dixie."

3

As we drove off the highway, I looked up and saw several crop-dusting planes jettisoning their payloads all over the place. A powder-blue Cessna AgWagon swooped low right over us, spraying the mist that I wiped with my sleeve from my mask's shield. Horses and cows lay motionless in pastures. Squirrels fell from branches. Birds dropped from the sky. Some birds fluttered down, staggered, then fell over. Some fell like stones. We passed a couple of shacks, the shotgun type, set up on square brick standards at the corners. People lay motionless on one of the porches.

"What's going on?" I asked.

"Nappy time," Sill said.

We drove past two incapacitated coyotes on the side of the road. "Are they dead?" I asked.

"Of course not." A black bird, perhaps a crow, crashed onto the hood of the jeep and bounced off into the brush at the side of the road. "Well, that one is. Generally speaking, though, they're all just sleeping. Even the ones a couple of rungs down the evolutionary ladder."

I looked at him through my foggy shield.

"The hillbillies."

"Oh."

"They'll wake up wondering which of their cousins they screwed and the planet will keep on spinning and tilting. However, I don't want you to think that my passion for killing is waning." We approached a guard's station set into a three-meter-high razorwire fence. "Give me your sidearm," he said, holding his hand back and open to one of his men. He took the pistol that was handed to him and put a bullet through the forehead of one of the sleeping guards.

Eigen screamed.

Sill smiled inside his mask. "See. Same old me."

I think I peed a little.

He handed back the gun. "I hate those things," he said. "So heavy. So loud. Didn't you think that was loud?"

Sill led the line of vehicles through the gate and onto what I assumed to be the grounds of Fort Knox. The road twisted through a forest and opened up to be an expanse of exercise yards and shooting ranges. Soldiers were strewn everywhere, lying on the ground, draped over monkey bars, slumped over Hummer hoods, and one unfortunate soul who had been engaged in hand-grenade drills lay in pieces.

"I know what you you're thinking," Sill said. "You're thinking, Are we there yet? And the answer is no. Another two miles across the base. How are we doing back there?"

There was no answer.

To me he said, "Pretty exciting, right? To think that soon we'll be opening that giant vault and there it will be. Nothing. I'm absolutely beside myself with excitement. No, wait, that's you." He yukyukked. He had never actually seemed insane before, but he did at that moment. "It's not much of a fight when the enemy is asleep, but don't look a gift nothing in the mouth."

The depository came into view ahead of us. It was larger than I had imagined. Sill waved for an armored vehicle to come up from the rear. It was an APC with a small cannon on the top. It stopped beside our jeep and Sill pointed forward. "Just ram it," he shouted.

He looked at me. "I enjoy the cannon, but it's even louder than the pistol. And it's messy."

The APC rolled forward toward the guardhouse. It had a rear bumper sticker that read *Legalize Recreational Plutonium*. The vehicle simply ran over the guard station and the fencing around it. The driver did so without regard for the helpless and harmless soldiers lying about asleep. I found I couldn't watch and so I looked back at Eigen. Her eyes were tightly shut and she was shaking.

"Keep them shut," I whispered, knowing there was no way she could hear me.

"Forward!" Sill shouted inside his headgear and pointed, just like a cowboy leading a wagon train.

The armored vehicle stopped at the giant front doors of the installation. Sill turned to me. "You might want to cover your ears. The cannon is necessary now." He covered his own ears. I gestured to Eigen to do the same.

My hands over my ears did little to block the percussive force of the gun. I wondered what it would have been like had I not covered up. The door to the building was obliterated; only a cartoonish gap was left in the face of the structure.

Sill got out of the jeep and waved for his men to surround the building, this while the crop-dusting Cessna made another pass.

I followed Sill inside. It was just the two of us. The edges of the blown-away door and walls were still smoking. The sounds of engines, land and air, ceased and an eerie silence sat with us in the rubble. The building was surprisingly old fashioned inside, lots of oak paneling, marble surfaces. We walked through the smallish foyer, through double doors into a large room with no counters or surfaces, but with two machine gun nests, complete with machine guns, on either side of impressively large metal doors that stood closed under the word *Vault* etched into the marble wall.

I looked at the sleeping solders lying near their weapons. "This is it?" I said. "This is the security of Fort Knox?"

"Perceived security is as good as the real thing," Sill said. "No one thinks to rob what is known to be the most heavily fortified place on the planet."

"You did."

"Well, I'm different." He looked at his watch and removed his mask. "It's okay, you can take it off now."

I did. I detected the faint odor of lilacs.

"It's fine," he said. "The fragrance will persist for a while, but the effect will last for several hours. Let's get into this thing."

On the vault door, with all its metal rods and shafts and massive hinges, there was a combination lock. Not a surprise, but the lock was set just about a meter and a half off the floor and looked very much like the dial one might find on a gym locker.

Again, I said, "This is it?"

Sill laughed. "Genius."

"I suppose you know the combination."

"Alas, poor Takitall. He's not here to do the honors, but he did manage to scribble the digits down on this cocktail napkin."

4

"Let me see," Sill said looking at the napkin. "Twenty-four left, twenty-four right, and twenty-four left." He pulled down the handle and the door clicked open.

"You had to read that from the napkin?" I asked.

"No, but it looked cool, right?" He grabbed the huge metal handles and pulled. "A little help," he said.

I pulled with him. The doors were enormous, two and a half meters high and perhaps three wide. The hinges were apparently well oiled as they didn't complain at all. When one door was pulled open, we stepped back to see.

"Fucking shit," Sill said. "Goddamn, fucking shit, motherfucker, cocksucker, ass eater, fucking goddamn shit."

The vault was stacked floor to ceiling with gold. The vault interior appeared to easily extend back more than fifty meters. It looked like a perspective demonstration, the gold gleaming under bright lights converging on a single point so far away.

"It's just fucking gold." He looked at me. "Goddammit."

"You're rich," I said.

"I was already rich."

"Richer," I said.

"Don't fuck with me, math man." Then he stopped. He was attending to something in the vault. "Oh, my," he said. "What do we have here?"

I could see what he saw. He went inside and came back with a shoebox. It was a blue box with a white stripe and written on it was *P.F. Flyers*. The lid was held fast with string.

"This is it, Wala," Sill said. He gently shook the box near his ear, smiling. "Nothing is in here."

I said nothing.

"Nothing, Wala." He considered it. "It's heavier than I thought it would be." He pushed it toward me. "Feel it."

I took it from him. The box did feel heavy, though it also felt empty.

Sill took it back. "Nothing, right?"

I shrugged.

"Skeptics," he said. He pulled out his radio. "Bring in the trucks and get this gold out of here."

"So you did want the gold," I said.

"Can't just leave this stuff exposed like this. What kind of villain leaves thirty trillion dollars in gold bars behind? Not this villain."

We walked outside. A helicopter had landed. It was surrounded by men in black suits. In the middle of them was the nearly albino Vice President Shilling. His face was a smile and never did anyone look eviler to me.

"Nice, Mr. Sill, nice."

"I thought we had wasted our time," Sill said. "That vault is full of gold. But this box, this box is what I want."

"What's in it?" Shilling asked.

"Nothing, of course. You really don't get it, do you? This has always been about nothing. And now I have it."

Shilling stared into the building. "It's really full of gold?"

"Yes," Sill said, dismissively.

"What now?" Shilling asked.

"Well, first, I'd like to thank you and the senators for all of your help."

Shilling looked around. "Where is Takitall?"

"Somebody sort of killed him."

"You killed him."

"No." Sill shook his head. "Nor did I have him killed. I sort of liked the good general. But I could have killed him. That wouldn't have been a big deal."

"You're crazy," Shilling said, affectionately.

Sill nodded. He put a finger in the air, a signal. Gunfire rang out and all of the Secret Service agents and the marines at the helicopter fell to the ground.

"But I don't like you," Sill said to Shilling. "You bother me. You're like a walking flag. When you open your mouth, I hear the anthem."

"You fool, I'm the vice president."

Sill held out his open hand and his man who had sat with Eigen ran over to give him a WWII-era German Luger and without another word Sill shot the vice president of the United States through his right eye, killing him.

"Sorry you had to see that," he said to me. He returned the pistol. "It's getting a little chilly. What do you say we head back to my house for refreshments? We can decide what we're going to do with this." He kissed the box.

Il n'y a pas de hors-texte

1

Back at Sill's house the shoebox sat on the central counter in the massive kitchen. There was a rack of some thirty bananas on the surface as well. Nothing else. Eigen, Gloria, and I sat at one end of the long bocote table while Sill paced. He stopped at the bananas, tore off a couple, and tossed them to Eigen and me.

"Bananas are good for you," he said. "These are Gros Michel. That Cavendish shit they sell in the markets are no good, tasteless. Smell that one." He pointed to the banana in my hand. "Now that's a banana. Fungus took the Gros Michel out."

The banana did smell delicious.

"Have you noticed that there are no seeds in a banana?"

"They propagate vegetatively," I said.

"You read a book about it," he said.

I felt strangely embarrassed.

He looked at Eigen. "He's right. No sex for the old banana. Ironic, right? Just a piece of the tree. Shame."

"Don't you think we should get out of here?" I asked. "Or you should get out of here? I mean, you did just shoot the vice president."

"Nobody gives a flying fuck about the vice president. Anyway, I hated that pigmentally challenged son of a bitch."

"I doubt the government is going to feel the same way."

"The government, Wala, doesn't feel anything. That bastard was willing to take all the gold he could back to whatever midwestern state he came from. Did you hear that? Shilling was willing. That would have made a great bumper sticker for his presidential bid. Now, about this box."

"I think there's something in it," I said.

"Yeah, nothing's in it."

"It's too heavy," I said.

"You know the weight of nothing."

"Well, no," I said.

"Then shut up."

"Hold it right there!" It was Bill Clinton. He and Mitchell stepped into the room, automatic rifles pointed.

"Bill Clinton," Sill said. "Not surprised to see you. Does my lack of surprise surprise *you*? And you've brought Miller with you."

"Mitchell," said Mitchell.

"Yeah, right."

"We'll be taking that box, Sill," Mitchell said.

"A comedian," Sill said. "And what do you think is in this box?"

"This is where it ends," said Clinton.

"You don't really think you sneaked up on anybody, do you," Sill said. "Coming in here with your weapons brandished, dressed like fucking ninjas."

"I would say that you're going to prison," Clinton said. "But you know as well as I do that you're on your way to the remotest, darkest black site there is."

"Quincy, Massachusetts?" Sill asked.

"What?" Clinton looked at his partner.

"You can't handle what's in this box," Sill said.

"We're the government, there's nothing we can't handle."

"Yeah, I know. This is nothing you can't handle."

"What?"

"There's nothing in this box."

"Whatever. We're taking you in."

"We're taking you in," Sill mocked Clinton. "You watch too many movies."

"He shot the vice president," Eigen said.

Clinton nodded. "We know. Nobody cares about the vice president. He was just the president's insurance policy. Anyway, we don't answer to any branch of the government. We just take care of business. So, if you turn around, we'll put the cuffs on you and we can be going."

Sill simply stared at them. "You seem to have a little something on your face. Is that a red dot?"

Clinton and Mitchell looked at each other, saw the laser dots on each other's foreheads, and dropped their weapons.

"Is this the part when you fill us in on your diabolical plan?" Clinton asked.

"No." Sill nodded and both men were shot dead. I screamed at being so startled. "Government," Sill chuckled. "Whose fucking government? Your government, Wala? Professor Vector, your government?" He looked at the dead men on the floor. "What a fucking mess. DeMarcus!"

DeMarcus appeared. He looked at the bodies.

"Tidy up in here, please," Sill said.

"Right away."

"I need to rest," Sill said. "I'm going to take my box to my room and take a rest. Gloria, take them to the basement."

"Yes, Mr. Sill."

"You really should have had sex with her," Sill said to me.

2

"Is it your plan to kill everyone?" I asked. We were in the library now. The P.F. Flyer shoebox was sitting on top of a pristine first edition of Twain's *Huck Finn*.

"They're the lucky ones," Sill said. "The rest, nothing will happen to. Which would you prefer?"

"Nothing is going to happen to no one," someone said. From behind a bookcase stepped my gender-ambiguous student Sam.

"Sam?" I said.

"Who's Sam?" Sill asked. "Who are you?"

"Sam is my student," I said. "How did you get here?"

"I'm actually from MI6," Sam said. "My name is not Sam. It's Chris."

"Sam, Chris, Jesus, it doesn't matter," Sill said. "This box has nothing in it and it's all mine."

"Sam," I said. "Chris, be careful. He's already killed several people."

"If I keep this up, I'll get a reputation," Sill said.

"But you've been in my class all year," I said.

"We knew this was coming," Chris said. He pointed a pistol at Sill. "The box."

"Actually, I'll take the box." DeMarcus stepped into the room, holding a pistol of his own.

"DeMarcus?" Sill said, incredulously.

"Xue Wenqing, MSS, China," DeMarcus said.

"I can't believe this," Sill said. "You've been with me for five years."

"I'm thorough," Xue said.

Eigen was smiling.

"What is it?" I whispered to her.

"This is crazy. I love it."

"Sorry, Chris," Xue said. "I was here first."

"I am not giving this shoebox to someone named Xue," Sill said. "Or Chris. Everybody's going to so much trouble over nothing. Well, it's mine, and if anyone takes another step I'll pull this string and open the box."

Xue and Chris froze.

"Lower the pistols," Sill said.

"What about mine?" This voice came from behind Sill. The voice belonged to Leon Coltrane.

"Mr. Coltrane?" I said.

"Yes," he said. "And my name really is Leon Coltrane."

"You're a hundred years old," Sill said.

"And yet my pistol is brand new."

"And who do you work for?" Sill was on the verge of laughter.

"Bundesnachrichtendienst, Federal Republic of Germany."

"I can't believe this. I am a villain. I mean, I am *the* villain."

"Where's Trigo?" Eigen asked.

Coltrane turned around to reveal Trigo's head poking out of a pack on his back.

Eigen rose to run to him. I pulled her back. "There are a lot of guns in this room," I said to her.

Sill rubbed the end of the bowstring of the box between his fingers. "What will happen if I open this box?"

"Nothing," I said.

"Nothing," Sill repeated. "Are any of you ready for that? Mr. MI6, Chris, Sam, whatever, are you ready for nothing? All your training has you ready for anything, but are you ready for nothing? Are you a double zero? I hope they sent a double-naught spy for me. Are you 007? 009?"

"Just Chris."

"How disappointing." He turned to Xue. "And you? Ready for nothing to happen? You come from a country of a billion people. Busy, busy, busy. Ready for nothing? And you, German guy. How do you people get through a sentence with words so long? What is it again? Bunderchristinatoilet? Are you ready?"

"There is *something* in that box," I said.

"That's right, Wala, that something is nothing."

"Not nothing," I said.

"And I say it's not not nothing, which makes it nothing. But we could do this all day." He looked at each one of us in turn. I was last. "Let's find out."

Sill pulled the string and the bow came slowly undone. The string ends fell away, seemed to float through the air. He grabbed the lid of the box, paused there, took a deep breath. In fact, I could hear all of us breathing. I looked at Eigen. She was shaking. I realized that I was, too. Sill removed the lid.

Nothing happened.

God help us. Nothing happened.

PERCIVAL EVERETT is Distinguished Professor of English at the University of Southern California and the author of over thirty books, including *The Trees, Telephone, I Am Not Sidney Poitier,* and *Erasure.*

The text of *Dr. No* is set in Dante MT Pro.
Book design by Rachel Holscher.
Composition by Bookmobile Design and Digital
Publisher Services, Minneapolis, Minnesota.
Manufactured by Kingery Printing on acid-free,
100 percent postconsumer wastepaper.